I0672966

Unsurpassed

No Rival, #1

Charity Parkerson

--Warning: This book is intended for readers over the age of 18.

Editor: Vicky Reese
Photographer: Wander Aguiar
Cover Model: Matthew Hosea
Originally published by Ellora's Cave Publishing under the
same title.

Introduction

Book 1 in the No Rival series

For months, Aubree has been obsessed with two men—best friends, Max and Ryan. She's resigned herself to having her desires be nothing more than a late night fantasy. When the pair invites her to a weekend party hosted by a famous MMA champion, Drew Alexander, she accepts without a qualm. She never expects the two men plan to make her secret longings into reality. Unfortunately, that's only half their agenda. When Aubree learns the men's true intentions, she turns to Drew for help.

Drew is unlike anyone she's ever met. He's fun and playful. Dark and brooding. He's everything she's been searching for rolled up in a delicious package. Unfortunately, Max and Ryan aren't finished with her yet. Aubree has to choose—does she cling to the friendship she's had with Max and Ryan, or risk everything on one man who could make all her dreams come true?

Chapter One

She could lick him. It wasn't a new thought for Aubree. However, it was one gaining the possibility of becoming reality with each passing moment. Sweat glistened on Max's skin. His gray cotton t-shirt stuck to his pecs. Her soaking panties clung to her. She could swipe her tongue across his skin and then keep walking as if nothing had happened. Knowing Max as she did, he'd most likely chalk it up to her quirkiness and let it go. At least then, she would know. She'd have the memory of his flavor to add to the fantasy she took to bed with her each night.

As she looked on, one massive shoulder lifted as he raised his arm to wipe the sweat away from his brow.

Aubree bit her bottom lip to keep from moaning. Almost as if he felt her stare, he turned in her direction. Their gazes collided across the room. Even though Max was too far away to make out the color of his eyes, she was as familiar with them as she was with her own. They were an odd shade of amber with specks of green scattered throughout.

Max didn't smile. He rarely did, but when it happened...it was magical. She wanted to run her hands over his short brown hair, allowing the soft bristles to tickle her skin. Hunger consumed her. A flush crept up her skin. It had nothing to do with strenuous exercise. Of course, she hadn't done a single leg press since claiming the weight machine. She'd been ensnared by watching the sexy kickboxing instructor do his thing. Now she couldn't look away from him and damn it, he knew it.

"How's it going, gorgeous?" Ryan's voice cut through her thoughts as his fingers brushed over her collarbone. Max turned away. Tearing her eyes from his wide frame, Aubree switched her attention to the man who'd claimed the weight bench beside her. Unlike Max, Ryan always smiled. She couldn't help but return the gesture.

"It's going okay," she answered as she soaked up his presence. With shaggy, dark hair and his skin covered in tattoos, Ryan was too easy to like. His sweet personality combined with his open smile was irresistible. If she could've chosen between the two kickboxing/self-defense coaches, she would have snagged one of them already—or gone to jail for stalking. Whichever happened first.

"Why are you looking so intense

today?"

Keeping her face carefully blank, Aubree feigned ignorance. "I don't know what you mean." His green eyes flashed with humor, making her wonder for a moment what he was thinking.

"You were staring into space," he said in way of explanation. Relief flooded her veins. He hadn't noticed her watching Max.

"I'm starving." It wasn't a complete lie. She was ravenous. Another knowing grin passed over his face. She beat down the blush fighting to rise in her cheeks. Ryan and Max both knew her too well. She hoped they didn't know everything.

"I could use something to eat as well. What would you like?" There was a moment when Aubree wondered if he was talking about food. In the end, she decided it was merely wishful thinking on her part when his expression didn't change.

"What are we talking about?" Max asked, appearing at their side. Ryan slid over, making room for him to sit.

"Eating out," Ryan answered.

A wicked smile touched Max's lips. "Really," he drawled as he held her gaze. Aubree's imagination fired to life once more causing her nipples to harden.

She opened her mouth to answer. Her voice came out in a squeak, forcing her to clear her throat. "Yeah. I'm thinking about skipping out of here early tonight."

Max's brow furrowed. "You don't want to try one quick private lesson before you go? I'm done with my classes and your balance is still off."

She hated to say no since the private lessons the pair offered her was how the three of them had become such good friends. It had taken one visit to their regular class to realize she did not possess the coordination needed for kickboxing. Most people would hear "one class" and think she'd given up too soon. That's because they didn't realize her single visit had ended with a sprained ankle, a black eye and a trophy case that would never be the same again.

As much as she wanted to say yes, the thought of either man pressing his hard body against her while pinning her to the floor caused Aubree to squirm in her seat. "I need a shower," she answered hastily, and a ride on my vibrator while moaning your name, Aubree silently added. Her channel pulsed in response.

"A cheat night? Sweet," Ryan said, sounding cheerful. "Give us an hour and we'll swing by to pick you up."

"Okay," Aubree agreed.

Ryan's eyes twinkled. "What? You're

not even going to ask where we're going?" Although it was on the tip of her tongue to say she didn't care, Aubree still felt a flush climb up her cheeks. "Where are we going?"

"To eat," both men answered simultaneously.

* * * * *

The moment Aubree closed her front door behind her, she couldn't strip off her clothes fast enough. The brush of material against her over-sensitized skin left her agitated. She headed straight for the shower, hoping to wash away the scorching fantasies running through her mind. No matter how cold she turned the water, the heat wouldn't dissipate. Giving it up as a bad job, she stepped out, eyeing the bedside table before glancing at the clock. The hour she'd been allotted didn't give her much time. If she didn't do something, Aubree feared her reaction to being alone with the men. It was only a matter of time before her longing for their touch would cause her mind to snap, and then what would she do? Most likely, she'd gain super-human strength, pin one of them to the ground and attempt to ride his face, while the other one tried to pull her off. She chuckled at the picture even as her pussy wept.

With a growl, Aubree swept her hand over her freshly waxed cunt as a shiver of yearning ran through her. Giving it up as a lost cause, she rushed across the room. She'd have to be quick, but she couldn't wait any longer. Opening the drawer next to the bed, she pulled out her bullet and an anal plug. If Ryan and Max knew how many times she'd played out this same fantasy in her mind, they'd never be able to look her in the eye again.

Crawling onto the mattress, Aubree drew her knees up as the image of the two men filled her mind. Ryan's laughing green eyes and Max's sensual mouth were in the room with her as she spun the dial to high on her vibrator. Touching the cold metal to her heated flesh, Aubree's back arched as her juices leaked from her slit, running down to the puckered strawberry awaiting its own toy. She didn't need much preparation. She'd been primed all day. Reaching between her legs, she slipped the plug inside her ass. Her body greedily accepted the intrusion.

Most women were satisfied with one man. Aubree longed for two. She wanted Max and Ryan to fill her with their cocks. In her mind, she pictured them doing that very thing as she spread her knees wide.

The bullet beat against her clit as she pumped her fingers inside her channel. Her ass pulled at the plug. A part of her brain recognized she was missing the real thing and cried out in denial as her body took what pleasure it could. Even as her legs shook and her channel pulsed with the power of her orgasm, she didn't stop. She wanted it again and again until she could drown out the empty place inside her where Max and Ryan belonged. Aubree moved the vibrator frantically over her button until a second wave hit. She cried out in pleasure. Her breathing was shallow and her heart raced as she came down from her high. Switching off her toy, she tugged at the plug, groaning as the move sent a pulsation through her.

Even after two powerful orgasms, Aubree wasn't satisfied. She wanted the real thing. As if her yearning called to them, a loud knock landed on her door and Aubree shot to her feet.

"I'm coming," she called. A high-pitched nervous giggle escaped with the words. If only they knew how true her words were. She shook her head as she dumped her toys back in the drawer, making a mental note to clean them later.

*

Aubree answered the door after a considerably long wait, wearing a short, silk robe and nothing else. A flush covered her skin. Her wet, blonde locks fell in a dripping mass over her shoulders. The thin material covering her body clung to her skin, shaping her every curve, doing nothing to hide her hardened nipples. It took every ounce of Ryan's willpower to keep his gaze at eye level. He held out the pizza box in hopes of distracting her from his growing erection.

"I brought food." Max gave him a push from behind to get him moving as the asinine comment left his lips.

Stepping aside, she waved them in. "Yum. I'm grateful we're not going anywhere. It's been a long day." While Max settled on the couch, and switched on the television, Aubree followed Ryan into the kitchen. He spoke over his shoulder.

"You said you were starving so we took you at your word."

He set the pizza on the stove and turned to find Aubree stretched up onto her toes, digging around in the cabinet next to the sink. The light-blue silk robe rode up. He stared at the outline of her barely covered ass. It wouldn't take more than a second to slip the material the rest of the way up, revealing the gorgeous skin hidden from him. With the idea at the forefront of his mind, he crowded her body with his as he reached past her and grabbed the plates she'd been after. Ryan kept enough distance so she wouldn't realize how hard he was for her, but he wanted to unsettle her a little. Aubree didn't disappoint. She glanced over her shoulder. When their gazes met, a blush exploded across her cheeks. He bit back a chuckle. It almost became a moan when her stare dropped to his mouth before returning to his eyes. The hunger shining out at him caught him off guard.

"You look as if you need me," he said, letting the words hang between them before adding, "to reach high things for you, I mean."

"Yes." Her response made him proud. She knew his game and was prepared to play. With a sigh of regret, he remembered Max in the other room. He moved away from his prey. As always, they chose informal dining at its best and Aubree settled onto the couch next to Max. Crossing her legs, she balanced her plate on her knee and took a huge bite out of her slice of pizza. Max timed his attack perfectly, waiting until her mouth was full before speaking up.

"Ryan and I have been invited to a three-day holiday-themed party this weekend at Black River Resort and Casino."

Aubree carefully chewed her food before responding. "A holiday party already? Sheesh. Thanksgiving is still two weeks away."

Ryan jumped in, nodding. "It's for charity so it's planned on a date least likely to interfere with anyone's plans with their family. The higher the attendance, the more money they're able to collect. There's supposed to be a ton of things to do there."

"Awesome. Have fun," Aubree said as she took another bite of her food.

"It's a yearly event thrown by Drew Alexander." Ryan didn't bother explaining who Drew Alexander was. He knew Aubree would know exactly to whom he referred. Her father had worked with UFC fighters before he'd been killed in a car accident five years earlier, and Drew was the biggest name in mixed martial arts.

"It's good he uses his fame to help others," Aubree said, still not showing the enthusiasm he hoped to see.

Obviously deciding she wouldn't be lured into anything, Max dove in with both feet. "We'd like you to go with us."

Aubree choked on her pizza, falling into a coughing fit. Max shifted uncomfortably while Ryan debated on whether he should beat her on the back.

Finally, after taking a huge swig of water from her bottle, Aubree managed to catch her breath. When she spoke, her voice came out sounding hoarse. "You want me to go to a party? For the weekend? With both of you?"

Ryan and Max nodded. Her gaze moved between them as if assessing the seriousness of their request. After a moment, she shrugged. Taking another bite, she spoke around a mouthful of food. "What the hell. You only live once."

Chapter Two

The outside of the Black River Resort and Casino was so brightly lit, Aubree imagined it could be seen from space. Everything in its interior gleamed, from the marble check-in counter to the wooden balustrades, all the way down to the tiny gold details twinkling at her everywhere she looked. Without a doubt, Aubree knew she would never be able to come up with the money to stay even one night in a place such as this on her own. This was a hotel and casino reserved for the highest of rollers.

Even though it was fifty-eight degrees outside, Aubree had still chosen a deep red, spaghetti-strapped, form-fitting dress for the evening. Not only did the outfit make her feel desirable, she expected the place would be hot as Hades after she'd consumed a few drinks. Not to mention all the body heat once people began crowding in. Ryan and Max looked sexy as sin in their black tuxedos. She'd spent the thirty-minute drive to the hotel staring at them both. It was exactly like stepping into a shoe store. When she stood inside a shoe store, she didn't know which direction to look first or what she wanted out of the trip. However, she did know how it would end—with a quick rush of euphoria followed swiftly by regret and a bill she couldn't afford to pay. Nothing good could come of this trip.

The party inside the casino was already in full swing, leaving little time for Aubree to explore the three-bedroom suite assigned to them for the weekend. Since she was a guest of a guest, Aubree automatically chose the smallest of rooms while Ryan and Max simply chose whatever they seemed to find most convenient. Everything was white, which she found odd. It made the room appear even more expensive and gave her extra faith in the hotel staff cleaning crew. Aubree couldn't imagine living in a place where she could stain anything at any moment. Tossing her purse on a settee near the bathroom, she did a quick lipstick and hair repair before heading out to claim her men.

The three met in the center of the suite. Ryan gave her a once-over. "Yep. You're still looking hot. Are you ready to get this show on the road?"

Aubree tugged nervously at the front of her low-cut dress, hoping against hope her overabundance of cleavage didn't become a nipple show before the end of the night. "Please let the alcohol be strong," she said in way of answer, causing Max to let out a husky laugh.

"We'll never find out from here." Ryan's reminder spurred Aubree into action and she headed for the door. With her nerves on edge, Aubree hoped for the sake of the rest of the partygoers she got at least one shot of tequila in her before anyone dared to wish her a Merry Christmas. She'd hate to punch some poor unsuspecting soul in the throat all because they didn't realize her parents had died on that day.

*

With the casino transformed from gambling hall to a winter paradise, it was obvious great care had been taken to ensure Drew Alexander's "holiday" party would offend no one. Everywhere Aubree looked, she saw a different culture represented. In one corner of the room sat several menorahs. In another, people sang while beating drums in celebration of Kwanzaa. Along one wall sat a huge paper horse and people were taking turns writing their names upon it. Max quietly explained it was a Hong Kong tradition. The horse would be burned on New Year's Day, carrying a list of wishes to the gods in its smoke. Even though Aubree found each tradition interesting in its own right, she still liked the Christmas tree in the center of the room the best. The gigantic tree reached almost to the ceiling and every branch held an assortment of ornaments. A train set circled the base of the spruce while a white rocking chair sat to its left. A brightly dressed Santa perched in the chair, smiling jovially at each passerby. Nostalgia swept over Aubree.

Glancing away from the man in red,

she found both Max and Ryan silently watching her. "What?"

"You seemed sad there for a minute," Ryan explained.

Aubree shook her head. "It's nothing. I was thinking about my dad. He used to dress up as Santa each year. I stopped celebrating the holidays after he died." She waved her hand at the pair when it looked as if they were about to begin spilling platitudes. "It's not a big deal. Please forget I said anything?"

Max's jaw hardened as if he bit down his words, but Ryan opened his mouth seemingly prepared to dismiss her wishes. Luckily, a wide-shouldered man with a bald head clapped him heartily across the back, interrupting whatever he'd been about to say.

"Hey man. I'm so glad you could make it."

To Aubree, Ryan's smile appeared forced as he returned the greeting. "Hey Drew. I wouldn't miss out on this freak show for anything." Max chuckled and Aubree groaned at Ryan's words. Their host turned his laughing gaze in her direction.

"And who is this enchanting woman you've brought with you?" Drew's question could've been aimed at either man. However, she couldn't have said which one since he held her ensnared as the inquiry left his lips. Oh what delicious lips they were. In spite of his bald head—which had obviously been shaved—the rest of Drew Alexander was overwhelmingly stunning. Gray eyes, full lips and deep lines at the corners of his mouth were a few of the weapons he held in his arsenal. His golden skin and the rumble of his voice completed the package.

Holding out her hand, Aubree introduced herself when neither Ryan nor Max jumped to handle the job. "I'm Aubree Holiday."

Drew's gaze dropped to where her feet touched the floor, before skirting up her body and coming to rest on her face. The blatantly sexual scrutiny left Aubree feeling as if he'd physically run his hands over each place he looked. Taking her hand between his much larger ones, he slid closer and lifted her knuckles to his mouth. His warm lips skimmed the top of her hand as he held her gaze. "Charmed." The word dripped with lust. He didn't let her go even when Max cleared his throat.

Aubree was the one who was charmed but nothing else. In spite of Drew's appeal, she recognized his type. She was female, breathing and therefore a target. He wouldn't remember her name tomorrow. Tugging her hand away, Aubree linked her arm through Ryan's since he was the closest. Max moved to flank her other side. "Thank you for inviting us, Mr. Alexander. Everything looks amazing."

A flash of humor and a bit more interest moved over Drew's features at her dismissal. "Please call me Drew, and thank you. This is my favorite time of year. Not to mention, Sunrise Children's Hospital is a wonderful charity. I enjoy finding unique ways to raise money for them. Which of these two belongs to you?"

The question caught Aubree unawares. She floundered as all three men stared at her expectantly. Taking her silence as an answer, Drew somehow managed to—once again—claim her hand. He was leading her away from her friends before she knew what was happening. She attempted to shoot a pleading look over her shoulder but Drew's massive form blocked her.

Giving in, Aubree allowed the sexy fighter to escort her to the paper horse. Pointing at the long line of people waiting to add their name, he said, "This is the perfect example. Each person in this line has paid a hundred dollars apiece to have their wish sent up to the gods."

Effectively distracted, Aubree's mouth fell open. "A hundred dollars? I won't even embarrass myself by telling you how many hours I have to work to earn such an amount."

A deep, husky laugh fell from Drew's lips. "I take it you don't plan to add your name."

"I think I'll hold onto my wish so I can eat for the next week."

"What sort of work do you do?" he asked, sounding curious.

"I'm an RN at Sunrise Children's Hospital." At her answer, Drew threw his head back in laughter. Aubree found herself smiling at his open humor. He dressed like a man used to living in style while surrounded by fake people, but he seemed completely guileless.

Snaking his arm around her waist, he drew her against his side as he bypassed the line and approached the women taking donations at the front. Blonde-haired and blue-eyed, each of the three women stood close to six feet tall. Aubree didn't doubt they all worked as professional models. Judging by the way they smiled at Drew, Aubree was also willing to bet they'd give it up for a night with him.

The girl in the middle was the first to speak. "Good evening, Mr. Alexander. How may I help you?"

Dropping his arm from her waist, Drew pulled a few bills from inside his jacket and handed them to the model. "Ms. Holiday would like to add her name."

The blonde cut her eyes in Aubree's direction and smiled. It wasn't as welcoming as the one she'd given Drew. Aubree understood. "Of course," she said tightly as she held a Sharpie out in Aubree's direction. "Please feel free to sign the horse anywhere you can find a blank spot, Ms.... Did you say Holiday?" she asked, sounding surprised. "Are you related to Claude Holiday? If you don't mind me asking," she added hastily.

The first genuine smile of the evening touched Aubree's lips. "Yes. He was my father."

Drew's eyes sharpened, but the model smiled brightly. "I knew you looked familiar. I was so sad when I heard about your parents' accident. It's Mandy."

At the mention of her name, all the pieces clicked inside Aubree's head and she found herself reaching out for the girl at the same time Mandy squealed. "I cannot believe it's you," Aubree said as she hugged her. "It's been so long and you've really changed."

Mandy fluffed her hair. "Well, you can't wear pigtails forever."

An irritated huff at her back reminded Aubree she was holding up the line. She stepped to the side. Drew followed patiently and Aubree explained. "Mandy's father worked as a prizefighter for Wright's Casino. My dad was his manager."

"I actually knew your father well," Drew said, surprising her. Mandy glanced behind her at the ever-growing line.

"I'm sorry. I have to get back to

work, but I'd love to catch up with you if you'll be here all weekend."

"I am," Aubree agreed. With a small wave, Mandy jumped back into the fray. Once they were alone, Aubree asked Drew, "You knew my dad?"

The cocky smile and laughing eyes Drew hid behind before this point were gone. In their place was a serious version of him she wasn't expecting. It made him seem older and—for some reason she couldn't explain—more appealing. "He was one of the few people I considered a real friend. Believe it or not, in my mother's day, she was a ring-card girl. When she turned up pregnant with me—out of wedlock—no one wanted anything to do with her, but your dad gave her a job pushing paperwork."

Realizing she knew exactly whom he referred to, Aubree asked, "Your mom is

Gigi Alexander?" When he nodded, she struck without thought, slugging him in the arm. "Shut the fuck up!" He chuckled and she gasped, horrified by her own actions. She reached over, rubbing the spot where she'd hit him absently. "Your mom used to sneak me candy when my dad would put me in time-out. Come to think of it, I really blame her for the ten extra pounds I can't ever seem to lose."

"I'll be sure to let her know."

It had been five years since her parents had passed away and even longer since she'd spoken to anyone outside her family about either one of them. The crowd around them fell away as Aubree stared up at Drew. "Wow. I can't believe how small this world is. My dad would've loved knowing Gigi's son has gone as far as you have." She allowed a hint of shame to leak into her words. "I have a confession. I wasn't looking forward to this event, but now I'm really glad I came."

*

The blue of Aubree's eyes twinkled as she made her confession. For a single moment out of time, Drew forgot where he was. "I commend your bravery for showing up. I'm sure it wasn't an easy decision considering the theme."

Aubree's smile turned into a sad one, making Drew regret the words. Aubree's father had been well known and respected in the fighting world. News of the car accident on Christmas day that claimed the lives of both Aubree's parents had moved quickly through the MMA gossip mill. Drew didn't want to dampen the mood, but he'd been moved to say something. Unfortunately, now he was almost desperate to bring the happiness back into her eyes.

"Just think," he said, allowing a bit of devilry to show. "If you hadn't shown up this weekend, you wouldn't have met me. That would've been a real shame for you."

Aubree narrowed her eyes, but her grin gave her away. She was ready to play along. "How do you figure?"

"You would've missed your chance to seduce me, and although I'm not easy, I'm totally worth every moment."

Her teeth sank into her bottom lip. Drew could see her fighting back her laughter even as her eyes danced with it. He wasn't content to let it stand there. "You'd better get started." He made a show of looking at his watch. "I don't know what time you usually go to bed, but I've only got a few hours left in me. Wine me, dine me," he paused and smiled roguishly. "Well, you know the rest."

Aubree threw back her head

laughing loudly, snagging the attention of everyone nearby. She covered her mouth when several people turned in their direction. Her eyes swam with tears as she stared at him accusingly. With a chuckle, he held his hand out to her, pouring on the charm. "I would be honored if you would spend some time with me this evening. I can't promise to behave, but as I said, I am worth it. Not to mention, I'm so good when I'm being bad."

She rolled her eyes but linked her fingers through his. Feeling triumphant, he led her toward the high-roller room. She leaned closer to him, lowering her voice for only him to hear. "Just so you know, I would totally rock your world."

He didn't doubt it, not for one damn minute.

* * * * *

Aubree had more fun in the few hours she

spent with Drew than she could remember having in years. He teased without mercy and gave her his full attention. At times, he left her breathless with laughter. The next minute, he simply stole away the oxygen from the room with his hot glances. By the time he walked her to her room, she was wondering why she'd spent so many months lusting after two men she could never have. Leaning against the cool wood of the hotel room door, she met his stare trying hard not to smile like an idiot.

"This was fun."

Drew's eyes flashed. "If you ask nicely, I'll let you take me to bed."

She shook her head at his antics. "What if I'm not feeling especially nice?"

Drew brushed his hand over her hip. "You're right. You did feel naughty," he agreed. Holding her stare, he bent closer, giving her time to protest his advance. The door opened at Aubree's back. If she hadn't hit the solid wall of Max's chest, she might have ended up sprawled across the floor. Tilting back her head, she took note of the angry expression on Max's face before switching her gaze back to Drew. His eyes danced with humor as he mouthed, "Denied," and Aubree slapped her hand over her mouth to smother her giggles.

"Have a nice night, Drew." Drew ignored Max's snarling words. "May I see you again?"

"I'd like that," she answered without hesitation. Max growled. At the sound, Drew flashed him a cocky grin before giving her a wicked version of it and turning away. As soon as he moved out of the doorway, Max slammed it closed, focusing his ire on her. She'd never seen him truly angry before now. She laughed nervously.

"Are you drunk?"

"No," she answered, incredulous. "I've had two glasses of champagne all night."

"Your face is flushed."

Aubree shrugged. "I'm happy. I had a good time."

Max prowled toward her. The hard set of his jaw caused a flutter of desire to run through her. "Did you forget who you came here with?"

Unable to think of a single retort, she shrugged again. "I'm young and single. Why shouldn't I enjoy myself?"

Max's eyes flashed dangerously. His tone had a bite to it when he spoke. "You are not single."

Words failed her in the face of his heated gaze. She knew there were a thousand arguments against his announcement. She couldn't think of a single one. His eyes swept over her body. Every place they paused cheered with happiness. Her nipples hardened, and her muscles tensed, anticipating his touch. With her focus completely ensnared by Max, Aubree jumped in surprise when the warm weight of Ryan's arm encircled her waist. Her heart raced.

"Whoa," Ryan said. "What's going on?" His calm tone went far in the way of soothing her panic. Ryan had always been the body whisperer. When he spoke, the smooth vibrations in his voice would run over the person's skin, relaxing their muscles faster than the world's best massage. Max switched his gaze to Ryan as he answered, saving Aubree from attempting to find the words for what had passed between them.

"Drew was attempting to steal our

girl. I was explaining to Aubree how she has plenty to keep her entertained already. She's no longer free to go elsewhere." Aubree didn't know what she expected Ryan to say, but when the silence stretched on, she looked over in an attempt to gauge his reaction. To her surprise, he didn't seem the least bit taken aback by Max's pronouncement. Instead, he merely looked thoughtful.

"I think we've been too patient with you," he said after a moment. Pulling out of his grasp, she faced off against him. "What are you talking about?" Even as the panicked question left her lips, Aubree realized she already knew the answer. She'd always known, really. She crossed her arms underneath her breasts, then dropped them to her sides as the lessons they'd taught her about being prepared for an attack filled her mind. The motion didn't go unnoticed by him. A quick smile passed over Ryan's lips.

"Are you telling me you didn't see this coming?" Ryan asked quietly. She held her tongue as she realized she couldn't force it to shape such a lie. Max pressed his large frame against her back, engulfing her in his embrace. Incapable of holding Ryan's stare with Max's erection pressing against her ass, she instead chose to focus on the tan skin of Ryan's chest. In her shock, she hadn't realized his shirt was unbuttoned, exposing his muscular torso.

"Tell me you don't want this," Max demanded and God help her, she could not. She opened her mouth to say the words, the ones ending this game before it began and ruined everything between them. No sound escaped. At her silence, Max's lips touched her bare shoulder.

Closing the distance between them, Ryan tilted her chin up with his thumb, forcing her to meet his gaze. Gone was the sweet Ryan she'd always known. In his place was a turned-on Alpha male intent on consuming her.

Her mouth went dry. She swore she could almost taste the lust hanging in the air. She heard the sound of her zipper sliding down. The dress she wore loosened. Her brain detached from reality. Max's hands pushed the straps of her dress down her arms and his palms smoothed over the skin in their wake. His touch scorched her even as Ryan's mouth descended upon hers. When his tongue boldly stroked hers, her mind snapped out of its reverie. She realized her hands now clutched the lapels of his open shirt dragging him closer. She was beyond reason, and living in a place where her body reigned supreme. There was no going back.

Ryan held her face gently between his hands. The devouring kiss belied his soft touch. Max's teeth nipped at the skin of her neck before he brushed his tongue over the spot as if in apology. She didn't know which way to move as her mind went into overload from the sensations of her body. Flattening her palms against Ryan's chest, she hummed in delight over the hardened muscle beneath her fingertips. Impatience reared its head as she swept her hands up his chest and over his shoulders, pushing his shirt down his arms. Max's touch fell away for a moment. A cool breeze touched her bare skin making her realize he'd somehow divested her of her clothing while she'd been distracted.

Ryan's lips moved from her mouth

to her throat. Max buried his hand in her hair, tugging until she tilted her chin back far enough for him to take over. If she had believed Ryan's kiss to be intense, it was nothing in comparison to Max's bruising consumption of her lips. She couldn't breathe. There were too many mouths, too many hands, too many fingers. Max cupped her breasts between his hands, kneading them gently, as his hot erection probed at the globes of her ass, proving his clothes had gone the same way as hers. Ryan's teeth scraped along her stomach as he dropped down to his knees, kneeling at her feet. Max held her tight against his chest, as her feet left the floor. Ryan's mouth opened wide over her dripping cunt. With her thighs on Ryan's shoulders, she kept a hand buried in each man's hair as she fought to hang on to some form of control.

This was her ultimate fantasy come to life. She struggled to hold reality at bay. Ryan's tongue slipped inside her channel and he growled against her mound. "Damn, you taste fucking delicious." At his words, Max ripped his mouth away from hers and sucked in a deep breath as if calling on his patience. She whimpered over the loss of his kiss. Her disappointment was quickly forgotten as Ryan took her button between his teeth, nibbling gently.

"She's ready," Max announced, and Aubree fought back tears as Ryan set her feet back on the ground, denying her the release she sought. Bending at the waist, Max swept her into his arms. She instinctively wrapped her arms around his neck as he headed for Ryan's room. Catching a flash of a box of condoms on the bedside table, she realized they'd been prepared and waiting for her.

Ryan stripped out of the remainder of his clothing along the way while Max set her down at the edge of the mattress. Climbing onto the bed, Max settled back against the pillows and crooked his finger. Ryan placed his lips against her ear as he gripped her hips between his hands. Speaking quietly, he directed her movements. "Wrap your lips around his cock, but keep your gorgeous ass in the air for me. Understand?"

"Yes." Her answer came out sounding breathless. She didn't care. Ryan's controlling attitude gave her the freedom to do the things she wanted without guilt. Crawling up Max's body, Aubree paused to nip at his inner thigh. He sucked in a hiss. There was nothing soft about either man. They both spent their days inside a gym and the result of their hard work was Aubree's reward. All the dreams she had of licking Max were finally coming true. Gripping his shaft, she squeezed him lightly, lifting him toward her lips. A drop of semen leaked from the tip. She watched its progression in fascination.

"You're killing me, Aubree." His words shook her from the mesmerized haze. "I've been waiting for so long, baby. Let me feel your hot tongue."

Giving in to his demands, Aubree closed her mouth over his crown. The taste of male and salt exploded across her taste buds. She barely noticed the sound of Ryan ripping into the box of condoms. As the bulbous tip of Max's dick hit the roof of her mouth, Ryan's hips settled against her ass. His lips touched her spine. At the contact, Aubree sucked Max down her throat causing him to moan.

Ryan pushed inside her. The higher Aubree's lust skyrocketed, the bolder her motions became. As Ryan rocked against her, he encouraged her with words she could no longer hear. Her mind couldn't function beyond the needs of her body. When Ryan reached around, pinching her clit between his thumb and forefinger, Aubree bucked against his hand. His fingers were slick with her juices as he teased her button until the tingle exploded into an uncontrollable spasm. Aubree's orgasm caused her to tighten her throat around Max's staff as her inner muscles pulsed around Ryan's cock. A hot jet of semen filled her mouth. She swallowed against it. Max gripped her hair until her head stung at the roots. He pumped his hips upward, riding out the waves of pleasure. Ryan held her hips in place as he pounded against her. His fingers dug into her skin as he shouted loudly with his release.

Ryan collapsed against her, pinning her between him and Max. Almost as if by rote, Max and Ryan both rolled to their sides pulling her between them. Cradled against Ryan's chest, Max buried his face in her breasts. She held his head there, enjoying the tiny sensations running through her as his lips touched her nipple. Her breath came out in harsh gasps. An overwhelming exhaustion weighed down her limbs. Closing her eyes, she gave up the battle against it.

It seemed as if she'd only dozed off for a moment before Ryan touched her shoulder, pulling her from sleep. Glancing at the bedside table, the red numbers on the clock proved she'd been asleep for around an hour. "Sorry, baby," he whispered, leaning over her. "I'm scheduled to teach a self-defense class this morning, so I've got to head out, but I'll be back in a few hours. I didn't want you to wake up wondering where I went."

Thankfully, she was too tired for any sense of humiliation to rear its head. "Okay," she answered sleepily as he bent to touch his lips to hers. Ryan took her bottom lip between his own, making no other move to deepen the kiss. It was a sweet moment, one filled with promise, and despite her exhaustion, hope filled her chest.

The only light in the room was streaming from the open bathroom doorway. Aubree used it to watch Ryan finish dressing. The muscles in his back flexed as he tugged a t-shirt over his head. A flutter began in her stomach. It seemed she would never adjust to having sexy men around her even after they'd been inside her. With one last kiss on her cheek, Ryan gave Max a pointed look, one that left Aubree curious. Any questions she had died on her lips as Max's arm fell across her side and he drew her backward into his embrace. Tucked against Max's chest with his warm breath fanning across her hair, Aubree's eyes fell closed once more.

* * * * *

Ryan was back before Max and Aubree had the chance to get going for the day. The previous night's events left him wanting more. The memory of Aubree's body tightening around his cock combined with the expression on Max's face as she took him down her throat, had him determined to recreate both reactions. There was nothing sexier than Max in throes of passion. Before he got the chance to lure Aubree back to bed, a knock landed on the door. He moved to answer it before the sound caught Aubree's attention. The last thing he wanted was for her to get dressed. Drew stood on the other side with his feet braced apart and his arms crossed over his chest. Since his friendship with Drew had landed them this weekend stay, Ryan decided to play nice. Pasting on a fake smile, he greeted Drew with such enthusiasm it seemed ridiculous even to him. "Hey man! What brings you around?"

Drew's eyes moved over his shoulder. Ryan knew immediately he was there for Aubree, and Drew's first words confirmed it. "Can Aubree come out and play?"

Ryan bit back a curse. Even though Drew's presence meant their plan was working, he wasn't ready to hand over Aubree quite yet. "You just missed her," Ryan lied blatantly. Drew seemed genuinely disappointed. Ryan didn't feel an ounce of guilt. Waiting would feed Drew's interest.

"Okay. Well, tell her I'll be here at noon tomorrow to take her to lunch."

Ryan held onto his smile by force of will alone. "Not giving her a chance to refuse, huh?" He worried that some of his true feelings bled into the question when Drew eyed him carefully. Ryan kicked his smile up a notch in compensation.

"You know me," Drew answered after a moment. "I'm ruthless when I want something."

With a promise to deliver Drew's message, Ryan slipped the "do not disturb" sign in place and locked the door. Max stood there, his shoulder leaning against the doorway of the bedroom. Ryan nodded toward the bathroom, before heading in its direction. Max tilted his chin showing he understood Ryan's signal before falling in step behind him.

The last wisps of steam from Aubree's shower hung in the air. She leaned close to the mirror swiping Chap Stick over her lips. Her wet hair fell in dripping waves down her back and the fluffy white towel wrapped around her body was the only thing hiding its beauty from sight. Ryan's dick hardened painfully at the first glimpse of her. It was always the same when she was around. The difference between this weekend, and every other day before it was, he no longer needed to hide his reaction to her. She met his gaze in the mirror and smiled.

"Did I hear someone at the door?"

Pushing her wet hair aside, he pressed his lips to the back of her neck. He smiled in satisfaction as chill bumps immediately covered her skin. "It was

Drew. He plans to take you to lunch tomorrow at noon," he answered, seeing no reason to lie. Turning in his arms, she met his stare questioningly.

"Am I going?"

With a tug at the towel, Ryan stripped it away from her body. His mouth went dry at the vision of her delicious curves. "Yes," he answered absently. "You're still allowed to have friends." Smoothing his hands up her sides, he encircled her waist, hauling her against him until he was sure she could feel his erection between them. "As long as you remember who this body belongs to now."

*

Inside Aubree's mind, she was screaming for more. Catching sight of Max standing quietly in the open doorway, she met his hooded gaze over Ryan's shoulder. "Are you afraid?" Ryan asked against her ear.

"Of what?" Although Aubree felt sure she did know what Ryan referred to, a naughty part of her wanted to hear him say the words. He didn't disappoint.

"We'll both be inside you at the same time. If you don't think you can handle it, then I want you to tell me. We can take this slow." Lifting his hand, he absently stroked the skin at her collarbone as he continued speaking. He watched the motion of his fingers as if enthralled. "Neither of us want this to be painful for you, and I promise it won't be."

"Have you ever noticed this is your go-to move?"

Ryan's heated gaze moved from where his fingertips brushed along her collarbone to her eyes. His brow furrowed. Confusion was written in the lines of his face. "What?"

Aubree pointed to where his palm

rested near her shoulder. "As long as I've known you, you've always touched me in the same spot, no matter what we're discussing."

His face cleared and a small smile played upon his lips. "You're beautiful," he said as if it explained everything. "I always want to touch you, but right here...," He ran the tips of his fingers along the spot once more. "This is where I'm always imagining my tongue to be."

His reasoning shook something inside her, and Aubree realized she couldn't keep this up. She needed to know where this whole thing was heading. "What are the two of you doing to me?"

"Claiming what's ours."

She loved that Ryan didn't pretend to misunderstand her question or hesitate when he answered, but still, she needed more. "And this doesn't bother you? You don't feel jealous or expect I will eventually choose one over the other?"

He tilted his head to one side, assessing her. "Can you choose?"

"No."

"Even after last night?"

"Especially after last night," she answered honestly.

The tiny grin hovering on his lips grew into a luminous smile. "Good. We don't want you to pick between us. What'll it hurt to give us a shot?"

"Honestly? It'll hurt a great deal if this ends with me never seeing either of you again."

"Let me rephrase my question. What do you have to lose?"

She knew what Ryan was trying to say, and she didn't have any intentions of walking away from whatever was happening, but she still spent a second looking back and forth between the men. She wanted to scream her fear of losing their friendship. In the end, Aubree held her silence. Max's muscular bare chest and Ryan's soothing touch were stealing away her good sense. Everything else was secondary to having them inside her. It wasn't love. It was a raging desire to experience the sensory overload only they could provide.

Instead of answering Ryan's question, Aubree ran her fingertips over his abs as she brushed past him. Holding her head high, she headed for his bed. Halfway there, Max overcame her. Wrapping his arms around her waist, he lifted her feet from the floor, rushing her along. Max pressed his mouth to her ear. "I won't hurt you." As if accentuating his words, he cupped her mound, and ground his palm against her clit.

With his one touch, she was already panting. With his fingers moving over the spot where she wanted him the most, Aubree rode out the sensation while enjoying the sight of Ryan stripping out of his clothes. With protection in place, Ryan sat on the edge of the bed while reaching for her. Max gripped her hips, guiding her toward him.

"Max needs to get ready, baby. We have to keep you safe. In the meantime, I'll keep you company." The mischievous glint in his eyes had her straddling his hips without a second thought. She was drawn to the playfulness he always offered. His humor fell away on a moan as she sank down onto his cock. Ryan buried his fist in her hair, forcing her mouth to his. Nipping at her lips, he surged upward. The sweet spot at the apex of her thighs throbbed again with need.

Signaling his return to the action, Max flattened his palm between Aubree's shoulder blades, giving her a small push. At his cue, Ryan fell onto his back taking her with him. The sensation of Max's lips as they connected with the small of her back caused her to cry out in need. He traced a hot path up her spine until he reached her ear.

"You'll have to help me out." He ran his fingers over the entrance of her ass leaving behind cool moisture, making Aubree realize he was using some form of lubricant. The pressure of the head of his cock stretched her wide. It stung, but wasn't painful. "Rock back against me when you think you can take more of me." She did as Max instructed, conscious of how the pair filled her completely. The sounds coming from Max's throat drove her wild, making her feel powerful while

Ryan encouraged her to keep moving with his hands. Tilting her chin back, she let her head rest against Max's shoulder and allowed the men to control their pace.

"If you could see the way you look right now," Ryan said sounding more turned on than any man should. "So fucking sexy."

Max fingered her clit adding to the overabundance of sensations racing through her and sending her over the edge. Her muscles locked tight as someone gripped her almost painfully. She didn't care. It merely enhanced the awareness of her body. The echo of her name and the sweat slipping between them were memories she gathered closer to her chest. She hoped by the end of the weekend, she would have a thousand of those minute details to carry home with her, because she knew this couldn't last.

Chapter Three

Aubree stared at the dessert menu wishing she had the nerve to order something. There was no way in hell she was eating anything else in front of someone as fit as Drew. She'd been surprised to realize Mandy's usual position at the hotel was as a waitress. Having the girl's skinny model body hovering over her as Aubree lusted over the cake didn't help matters in any way.

"The chocolate is delicious," Mandy said as she filled Aubree's glass with water. "You should get a slice."

Aubree forced her face to remain blank. If Mandy had ever eaten anything sweet in her life, then Aubree was the president. She set the menu aside.

Drew's smile made her wonder if he

could read her mind. "Anything catch your eye? I mean, besides me, of course."

Before Aubree could answer, the glass of ice water Mandy held between her fingers slipped an inch, hitting the edge of the table, causing the clear liquid to sail out in an arc before splashing across Drew's shirt.

"Oh my gosh! I'm so sorry, Mr. Alexander," she cried as she flashed a wide grin in Aubree's direction with a wink. Aubree covered her mouth to hide her horrified laughter as she realized Mandy's move had been intentional. "Let me get a towel. I can't believe I did such a thing." She bustled away and Drew chuckled.

"Hmm, it seems we'll have to go back to my room so I can change. I might have to leave her a bigger tip for helping me get you alone." Not trusting her voice, Aubree tossed her napkin on the table and pushed her chair back, prepared to stand. Drew reached out halting her progress. "There's no need to rush. I don't mind spending a little time wet for you, if you'd like to try the chocolate cake. Especially if it means you'd be willing to spend time wet for me afterward."

The laughter Aubree managed to hold at bay up to this point burst from her lips without warning. "You're so outrageous."

Drew's wicked smile showed not a hint of remorse. "I didn't hear a 'no' in your statement."

Rolling her eyes, Aubree stood. "Come on. If you catch a cold because of me, there's no telling what you'll expect in return."

Aubree spent the elevator ride to Drew's penthouse doing her best not to stare at the way his wet, expensive button-down shirt clung to his skin. It seemed a night of wild sex had caused her hormones to rage completely out of control and now she was molesting every man with her eyes. Not every man, she conceded, only sexy fighters with too many muscles and an overabundance of charm. When the door slid open, Aubree all but leapt from the small moving room. She couldn't stand another moment trapped inside with Drew oozing testosterone. As if he could read her mind and had decided to challenge her self-control, Drew was out his shirt before she could blink or look away. She blamed the lack of warning for her reaction when her mouth fell open at the sight of him. His body went beyond all description. It should've been illegal.

"Damn you're sexy when you blush."

As the words fell from Drew's lips,

Aubree realized she was up against a seduction expert who was totally out of her league. Somehow, he managed to pitch his voice in such a way that she felt as if he'd growled against her ear while he was fucking her. It was easily the most sexual experience she'd ever had fully clothed, and she forcibly turned her face away to keep from doing something she couldn't take back.

"You don't fight—" Aubree froze mid-sentence as she caught sight of the man coming out of the bathroom. "Max?"

Max's steps faltered and he shot a nervous glance around the room as if searching for an escape. A second later, Ryan stepped from another room appearing equally as trapped. "Ryan?" Aubree asked, feeling like an idiot, but unable to stop. "What are the two of you doing here?"

"I'd like to hear the answer to that as well."

Gone was the seductive tone. Aubree caught herself checking to see if she was still with the same man. The change from playful to poised-to-strike was extreme and Aubree was almost frightened of Drew for a moment, until his hand came to rest on the small of her back.

*

The anger over seeing the two men rifling through his things tested Drew's control. His first reaction was to make them bleed. The panicked look Aubree shot him brought him back in check. When he touched her back, her entire body relaxed. He hoped it meant she understood his anger wasn't directed at her. He could tell by her reaction, she was every bit as surprised by the men's presence in his room as he was. Unfortunately, touching Aubree had the opposite effect on Max.

"You didn't waste any time jumping in bed with him. All it took was a free lunch."

Aubree drew back as if she'd been slapped as Max's strike hit its mark. Even Ryan flinched at the accusation. She didn't attempt to defend herself. The pain flashing across her eyes made Drew want to snap Max's neck, but since it had been Drew's intention to use every trick in the book to lure Aubree to his bed, and she was perfectly free to do as she chose, he couldn't understand Max's venom. The only thing Drew could think of was that Max was trying to turn Drew's attention away from him.

Running a tired hand across his eyes, Drew sighed. "I need a new shirt before I can deal with this shit." As quickly as possible, he dashed inside his room and slipped a cotton t-shirt over his head before returning to the sitting room. In his absence, Ryan and Max had taken over the chairs on one side of the coffee table while Aubree sat alone on the couch opposite them. Filling the empty spot next to Aubree, Drew draped his arm over the back of the settee. He intentionally kept his pose relaxed while also making a physical connection with Aubree. He didn't want either man to mistake his aims toward her. If this was a case of Max attempting to play the jealous lover, Drew was up for the challenge, and he always won.

Max's eyes followed the line of Drew's arm until they came to rest on where his fingers brushed Aubree's skin. Drew cleared his throat to bring Max's attention back to him. He raised his eyebrow in question. "I think you need to explain what you're doing here before I lose my patience."

Dropping his gaze to his knees, Max brushed his hands over his thighs as if nervously searching for the right words. "My dad has dementia," he said after a moment, and Drew slid down in his seat, propping his boot on the table in front of him as he recognized this would be a longer explanation than he first thought. "He took a turn for the worse about a year ago," Max continued. "And I couldn't take care of him any longer so he went to live in a nursing home. Anyhow, not long afterward, I went to visit him and we watched one of your televised events. You won the match by submission thirty-seven seconds in. It was impressive. Dad flew into this excited rant over how proud he was to have you as a son."

A terrible sense of foreboding overcame Drew. He ground his back teeth together. Max kept up his story as if he hadn't dropped any bombs on Drew's life. "At the time, I brushed it off as one of his not-so-good days, but then he kept talking about it every time I came to see him even at the most lucid of times. The more details he gave me, the more I wondered if he was telling me the truth. I started looking into things and it turned out everything he said added up. As much as I wanted to deny he'd cheated on my mom, I couldn't ignore what I'd learned."

Unlocking his jaw before he cracked a tooth, Drew did his best to sound reasonable. "None of which explains why you are here in my room."

Max dipped his chin, acknowledging Drew's impatience. "Six months ago, three things happened simultaneously. It seemed almost serendipitous. Dad asked why you never came to see him, Ryan met you while trying to drum up membership for our self-defense courses, and Aubree signed up for our kickboxing lessons."

Drew felt Aubree's muscles tense beneath his fingertips. He had to force himself not to look over to gauge her reaction. "So," Drew drawled, unable to believe what he was hearing. "You broke into my room hoping to find what exactly? DNA? A memento? And how exactly did you get in here?"

Max nodded. "Any of those things, and Ryan slipped a key out of a maid's cart early yesterday morning."

Drew's temper hitched up a notch. "Why the hell didn't you ask me directly? Seriously? It's not as if I fathered your child or some shit like that so why would I care?"

"Honestly? In your place, I would suspect anyone who claimed ties to me," Max admitted. "I would assume everyone hoped for some form of financial support and I didn't want that. I wanted to know the truth and as crazy as it might seem to you, this was easier than asking you openly or dragging anything out publicly. I can't imagine you wanting your mother's name in the news and I sure as hell don't want my family splashed all over every gossip column."

Drew spent a moment shaking his head as he attempted to come to grips with the elaborateness of Max's plan. Giving up, he said, "I'm not opposed to a private DNA test if it will get you out of my room."

*

While Drew and Max discussed plans for a DNA test, Ryan sat quietly watching Aubree. He knew the exact moment in which all the pieces of the puzzle fell into place inside her mind. She sat in frozen silence staring sightlessly at the corner from the moment Max made his dumbass comment about her sleeping with Drew. To the casual observer, she might've seemed fine. Ryan knew Aubree almost as well as he knew himself. This was hurting her deeply.

Although her expression never changed, one moment her eyes seemed almost unfocused and the next, the color left her face. She crossed her arms over her stomach as if attempting to hold herself together. His chest tightened. "No," he said before he could stop himself. Everyone froze, turning in his direction. He ignored them. Nothing mattered except for Aubree. "Whatever it is you're thinking, stop right there."

Aubree looked at Ryan as if noticing

he was there for the first time. The pain in her eyes left him feeling as if he'd been punched in the gut.

"Was this your plan all along?" she asked sounding broken. "Did the two of you—" Her voice cracked before she could finish her question, but Ryan knew what she meant.

"Aubree, we—"

"Just answer the question. Is this why the two of you invited me here?" With her holding his gaze, Ryan couldn't lie to her. "In part, but—"

"Oh my God," she whispered, cutting him off. "Why would you do such a thing? I thought—" She stopped again, shaking her head as if she couldn't go on.

"It's not what you're thinking," Max jumped in. "Yes, I hoped Drew might confide something in you he wouldn't tell anyone else, and we needed someone to

80

keep him distracted, but you know we care about you."

"No. I don't. You could've come here alone this weekend. You could've popped into this room while Drew was distracted by some other woman. It wasn't necessary for you to use me like this."

Max was shaking his head before Aubree finished speaking. Ryan was watching the whole thing unfold with a growing sense of dread.

"I needed to know, Aubree," Max admitted quietly. "This is important to me, and he's had a thousand women," he said with a wave in Drew's direction.

"A thousand is a bit much," Drew said drily, but everyone ignored him as Max continued pleading his case.

"Not just any woman would have held his attention for very long. Not the way you would, and we needed to know the exact times this room would be empty. We needed a woman we could control."

Before Max could say anything more, Aubree shot to her feet. "Control," she repeated and Ryan groaned at the rage she managed to project in a single word. "I see," she mused aloud sounding entirely too calm. "I have a connection to one of Drew's old friends and his family, making me a bit more interesting to him than other women. Of course since I've also been desperate to have you both in my bed, then I was easy pickings."

Drew's eyebrows rose at Aubree's statement. He stood clearing his throat. "I've heard enough. Would you like a ride home?" he asked, holding his hand out for Aubree.

With one last searching look at them both, Aubree switched her attention to Drew. "All of my things are still back in my room."

"Is there anything there you can't live without for now?" She shrugged. "I don't believe so."

"I'll have someone deliver your stuff to you later," he told her gently before turning a hard gaze on them. "I assume you know the way out, and I feel moved to warn you, your every move has been recorded from the moment you stepped off the elevator. Did you really think I wouldn't have some form of security?" As if punctuating how much he didn't care about their answer, he turned away taking Aubree with him.

Ryan wanted to demand she stay and wanted to beat the hell out of Drew for taking her away, but his guilt kept him glued to his seat. She was wrong. It had gone badly, but they did care about her. The weekend hadn't only been about finding out the truth. They could've proceeded with their plans for Drew without touching her. He couldn't say any of those things to Aubree because he'd felt the exact moment her trust in them died.

*

In a numb haze, Aubree held onto Drew's hand, wondering with whom she was the angriest. When the doors closed on the elevator, Drew pulled a phone from his pocket and even as his thumb moved over its face and he pressed it to his ear, he absently stroked her hand.

"Hey, it's Drew. I need my car."

Aubree listened to the short conversation with half an ear, and wasn't surprised when, by the time they made it outside, a silver Aston Martin Vanquish sat waiting for them at the curb. A smiling valet handed over the keys. Drew held open the passenger side door for her while she slid inside before circling around to the driver's side. It was impossible to block out the $300,000 luxury surrounding her as the door closed behind her. There were so many dials and buttons on the console between them, she couldn't even begin to guess the purpose of each one. Giving up, Aubree chose to focus on the man behind the wheel. He must think the worst of her.

"Where am I headed?"

The sound of his voice caused her to glance away guiltily as she realized she'd been staring. She rattled off her address. With his eyes on the road, Drew nodded. "I know the area."

Aubree spent the ride staring out the window and doing her best to block out everything. The level of deception was more than she could fathom. When her tan and brick condo came into view, she experienced a mixture of dread and relief at the sight of it. Her public degradation was at an end while the time alone with her thoughts was only beginning.

With the car in park, Aubree made no move to leave. Drew ran his hand around the steering wheel as if searching for the right words. Finally, he said, "So, Ryan and Max, huh?"

Humiliation sat heavy in her gut, but she refused to let it show. "Yep. Wow, I feel like a tramp admitting such a thing aloud."

Drew held his hands up in surrender. "No judgments here, seriously," he added when she cut her eyes at him skeptically. "Women come easily to me. I don't say that to sound conceited. It's part of the whole champion package. They don't really want me for me. It's usually only women who want to say they've shared my bed. But the point is,

I've done some wild shit in the past, and I'm not opposed to doing so again in the future."

Aubree snorted out a laugh at his confession before making one of her own. "I feel like an idiot. 'Control me.' He said those exact words. I want to go back and punch him in the throat."

"Understandable, but you know you could always get your revenge by having your way with me."

She shook her head in disbelief as she muttered, "Men."

Drew shrugged. "Hey, we're doers."

In spite of the weight sitting on Aubree's chest making it hard for her to breathe, she couldn't help but giggle over his antics.

"You laugh, but I'm serious. I'm more than willing to fall on the grenade here and let you use my body."

Aubree covered her face to hide the blush creeping into her cheeks. A masculine chuckle sounded from the seat beside her and she dropped her hands. "I'm sorry," she told him with her heart in her eyes. "I realize this day has been crazy for you too, and my shit is petty drama in the shadow of you learning you might have a brother."

Drew leaned his head against the headrest behind him and a serious expression settled on his face. "I've always known there was a possibility of a family out there. As a kid, I had this fantasy where my dad was some superstar who would show up one day and give my mom the life she deserved. Of course, I grew up and reality set in. I realized whoever he is, he's a douche."

"Yes he is," Aubree agreed without hesitation. "How could he be anything else if he left someone as amazing as you?" Feeling as if she'd said too much, Aubree glanced around uncomfortably. "Well, thanks for the ride home, and I hope everything works out." She reached for the door handle in hopes of making her exit before she made things any more awkward.

Drew called out stopping her. "Hold on a second." Fishing around in the console between the seats, he came out with a pen and a scrap of paper. He scribbled a few numbers on it before handing it over. "Here's the number to my cell. Call me if you need anything or even if you don't," he added with a hopeful smile.

Taking out her phone, Aubree dialed the number he handed her and waited until she heard his cell ring before disconnecting the call. "There, now you have my number too." With a teasing smile, she added, "I would've written it down, but I'd hate for it to get lost in the pile of phone numbers you already have squirreled away." Throwing open the door, she called over her shoulder. "Don't forget to save it to your contacts so you can call me if you need anything...or even if you don't."

Without waiting for a response, Aubree darted for the house. She realized too late her keys were back at the hotel, but luckily, she kept a spare under a potted plant outside. Her front door barely closed behind her when her cell phone chirped alerting her of an incoming text. Glancing down at it, she read Drew's message. "Max wasn't wrong about one thing. No other woman would've held my attention the way you did, and it had nothing to do with your father."

* * * * *

Aubree thanked her lucky stars she'd already asked for Monday off as she lounged around the house wearing nothing but an old pair of boxers and a ribbed tank top. Along with her house keys, the keys to her car were wherever her things currently sat. She flipped through the channels, cursing the name of whoever chose what aired on daytime television before finally giving it up as a bad job. With the silence closing in on her, Aubree stared at the phone wondering whom she should call to get her bags. Every name that came to mind, she immediately dismissed. With her concentration fully engaged, she jumped in surprise when a solid knock landed on the front door. Glancing down at her grungy clothes, she automatically felt the messy bun at the crown of her head and let out a loud groan.

When the tap came again, she sighed, and moved to answer. Going up on her toes, she checked the peephole, which caused her to groan louder. With no other options, Aubree threw the door open. At ten in the morning, the air outside was chillier than she would have liked, and her nipples hardened against it, reminding her of her braless state.

Thankfully, Drew kept his gaze eye level. "Good morning, beautiful. I thought you might need these." He held out her bag and purse.

"Thank you," she said automatically as she relieved him of his burden and stepped back enough for him to enter.

As she closed the door behind him and set her bags aside, she watched his expression, wondering what he was thinking. She knew he'd been raised by a single mother and most likely didn't live in the height of luxury back then, but nowadays he was accustomed to a much higher lifestyle than what he was currently standing in. Without waiting for an invitation, he plopped down on her tan sofa, settling in as if he intended to be there for a while. His masculine form seemed almost out of place in the center of her feminine home. The light yellow walls, delicately made wooden side tables, and small sofa appeared miniscule with his large presence filling the room. He gave the empty spot next to him a pat, leaving her with no other choice than to join him.

"I appreciate you bringing my things by. I didn't realize until I got home I didn't have anything in my pockets other than my phone and the keycard to the room. I was beginning to wonder how I would to get to work tomorrow." Even though she knew everything she was saying was reasonable, for some reason she couldn't explain, she felt as if she were rambling. His long, denim-encased legs took up too much space, forcing her thigh to press against his.

"I could've had someone bring your bags by last night, but I made a few calls, rushing things along. I took the DNA test this morning, and I wanted to be the one who delivered your stuff to you."

Turning her head and bringing him into her line of sight, she realized he was watching her closely as if gauging her reaction to his words. "Why?"

The gray of his irises seemed to sharpen and she found herself fascinated. "Well, as I recall, you were there. Max went to an extreme to get that test."

"No," she said interrupting him. "Why did you want to come here?"

"I needed to see you again." At his admission, she dropped her gaze. Unfortunately, it landed on his stomach. His white cotton t-shirt clung to his skin, outlining his well-defined abs. Lifting her eyes to his chest, she regretted it immediately as the dip between the flat pads of his chest held her in thrall. He said he "needed" to see her, not wanted. She hadn't missed the difference.

"Oh," she said for lack of anything more intelligent. Drew reached over and touched her chin forcing her to meet his stare.

"Are you okay?"

"I'm glad you came," she said instead of answering. He dropped his hand and glanced around the room.

"So," he drawled sounding uncomfortable for the first time. "What do you do for fun?"

The change in topic caught her unaware and she searched her mind for something to say. For the life of her, Aubree couldn't think of a single thing. "Well, I was taking private kickboxing lessons with Max and Ryan, but I guess those are over now," she finally said, since she had nothing else going on.

"I meant something you enjoy doing. That's not fun, but I can take over your lessons, so don't worry."

"I seriously doubt it," she said feeling moved to be honest. "I don't think I have the required balance. I haven't learned much in the past six months."

"As I said, don't worry over it. I'm better than they are, so you'll have it licked in no time."

Aubree shook her head in disbelief. "I can't decide if you're over-the-top conceited or if you're extremely honest."

Drew seemed to think it over. "Honest," he said after a moment with a decisive nod. "There're plenty of things I suck at, but you're changing the subject. What do you do for fun? How do you cut loose?" She shrugged, and he released a heavy sigh. "Come on. Your life can't be all work and paying your car note on time. There has to be some sort of hobby. When was the last time you did something completely ridiculous?"

With a self-deprecating smile, Aubree admitted, "Apparently when I go to a casino with my friends for the weekend, I lose my mind."

For the first time since he arrived at her door, a bright smile touched his lips, and it was as if she'd been given a gift. "I'm better at that as well. In case you were wondering." She huffed at his outrageous remark, but her heart wasn't really in it.

In truth, she knew Drew was being his usual self. She also didn't doubt every word he said was true. Slinging his arm across the back of the couch, he managed to move even closer. "I'm going to take you somewhere." He paused and his expression turned wicked. "Of course, you'll have to put a bra on first, though I'm not complaining," he quickly added. "I don't want everyone staring at what's mine."

"Yours?" She asked gearing up for a rant. "What is it with you men? You all want to claim ownership as if you were buying a car. Well, I don't care to be someone's possession to use as they please."

Instead of arguing, Drew smiled at her obvious outrage. "Don't worry. I have no problem with you using me in any way that brings you pleasure. Now go get dressed."

*

Drew held his breath, half expecting Aubree to tell him to leave. Fortunately, after a moment of assessing him with her eyes, she stood to do as he bade. He waited until she closed the bedroom door behind her before giving in to the triumphant smile growing inside him. Honestly, he wanted the opposite of dressed. The outline of her nipples showing through her shirt had tested him. However, persistence and patience were two qualities he possessed in abundance. She reminded him a lot of himself. Aubree was a tad naughty behind her distant façade. He would enjoy forcing her to expose it.

When the door leading into her bedroom opened again, Aubree reemerged wearing jeans and a long sleeved, form-fitting shirt. "I hope this is okay since you didn't say where we're going."

He let his gaze slip over her body making sure she felt its heat. "Perfect," he growled causing her to blush.

"Gosh. You're really on at all times."

He smirked at her grumbled remark. "How is it my fault you have a dirty mind? All I said was 'perfect'. You're the one who took it to mean you have an awesome body and I want to lick every inch of it, which I totally do by the way, but I didn't say as much."

The look on her face was priceless. It was a mixture of flattered and exasperated. She raised her hands and dropped them back to her sides as if she had no idea what she should say. "You make me want to scream."

He nodded his understanding. "Don't worry. You will. I can hear my name on your lips and reverberating off these walls already."

She tilted her head back and eyed the ceiling. He wondered if she was praying for patience, but when he heard a slight gurgle, he realized she was doing her best to hold back her laughter. When she finally dropped her chin, her eyes were shining, but her face was clear. "Come on. Let's go before I change my mind."

Even though he was sure she was joking, only the hint she might not leave with him got his feet moving. He was rushing her out the door as soon as her shoes were on. He didn't draw another easy breath until he had her in the car. It was a dangerous and unexplainable need driving him to be near Aubree.

It took ten minutes for Drew to make it across town, and when he pulled into the empty parking lot, he glanced over to see Aubree's confused expression. "Why are we at the park?"

"Because, whereas most people need to grow up, you, Aubree Holiday, need to learn how to play." He was almost certain she rolled her eyes, but she turned away before he could catch the gesture. With a snicker, he threw open his car door and jogged to the passenger side before she could open it on her own. She looked resigned as he helped her out of the car.

Walking backward toward the playground, he held onto her hands. "It'll be fun. I promise. Is this the face of a man who would lie to you?"

"Do you really want me to answer that?"

Drew's feet froze. Aubree walked into his chest. "Yes," he said, sounding serious even to him, but her answer was important. She studied his face giving him the impression she was carefully considering everything she knew about him before making her final decision.

Just when he thought he might snap, she finally shook her head. "You're not a liar. If anything, you're too honest."

The knot in his chest loosened, setting him free. A burst of happiness ran through his veins. "Good," he told her and without warning, he snatched her off her feet. Tucking her under one arm, he carried her like a football toward the swings.

"Holy shit!" She quickly covered her mouth at the screech, but it did nothing to hinder her peals of laughter.

Chapter Four

Ryan couldn't stop staring at him. Even for Max, he was brooding. He was always dark and moody, but this was different. He'd never seen Max in such a state. With his head resting on his fist, he leaned his weight on the arm of the couch, staring sightlessly at the corner of the room. They'd known each other since the day they both signed up for the Marines at eighteen. Ryan had stood by Max's side, through thick and thin, unwavering in his loyalty to his best friend. The white walls inside their apartment were closing in on Ryan making him feel as if he couldn't breathe. Unable to hold his silence a moment longer, Ryan burst.

"This is some fucking bullshit!" His skin felt two sizes too small and he wanted to crawl out of it. "We have to fix this.

Seriously, this is wrong. We were wrong."

As if Ryan's eruption was the motivation Max had been waiting for, he kicked the coffee table over in explosion of rage. With his outburst complete, Max's usual cold indifference fell back into place as he stood.

"Let's go." There was no need for Max to explain where they were going. Ryan snatched up his keys from the nearby kitchen table, following in Max's wake.

"It's about damn time."

It only took a few minutes to get to Aubree's. As her place came into view, Ryan spotted Drew's car pulling away from the curb. The flash of blonde hair in the passenger seat was unmistakably Aubree's. Without any plan in mind, Ryan followed the pair. He was aware his behavior bordered on stalker status, but he couldn't seem to make himself turn the SUV around. Max didn't question him. Ten minutes later, Ryan was seriously beginning to question his sanity. It was possible he could be following them to Canada for all he knew, so really, how long did he intend to keep this up? The moment he decided he was acting like an idiot, Drew pulled into the parking lot of the city playground.

Driving past, Ryan whipped into the next parking lot over, choosing a space where he could keep the pair in sight. Max held his silence and Ryan refused to look over to gauge his reaction. Out of the corner of his eye, he could see Max crossing his arms over his chest.

"I'm an idiot," he said when the silence dragged on a minute too long for his comfort.

Max shifted in his seat. "Sometimes

you do what you have to in order to get through the day. This is what we're doing to get through today."

He couldn't argue with Max's logic. Drew stepped out of the car, distracting Ryan from his thoughts. The giant fighter opened the passenger side door and helped Aubree out of the car. The way a real gentleman would, Ryan thought bitterly.

"He's smiling."

The sound of Max's voice cut through Ryan's brooding. "What?"

Max nodded in the pair's direction. "Drew. He's smiling. He never smiles."

Ryan leaned forward, peering closer at the couple as Drew walked backward holding onto Aubree's hands. Max was right. He couldn't remember seeing Drew smile often, but he was now. They stopped walking and the conversation seemed to turn serious for a moment before Drew's smile popped back into place. Ryan's heart sank as Drew scooped Aubree off her feet and took off running. Even from where they sat, and with the window rolled up, he could hear Aubree's laughter. When they reached the swings, Drew set Aubree on her feet. She turned in their direction for the first time as she sat down in the swing. Drew grabbed the chains and sent her sailing. She screamed as he let go of her, but Ryan couldn't miss her huge grin. He shifted into reverse.

"So, what now?"

Ryan shrugged at Max's question as he backed out of the parking space, doing his best to keep breathing. "Now, I do nothing. She's happy. All I could possibly do at this point is what I always do—fuck everything up."

Chapter Five

Drew pulled the hand wrap around his wrist a bit tighter then checked his range of motion again before circling his knuckles with the tape. He kept his focus locked on his task as he listened to Max. The familiar job kept the rage under control. When he'd been told he had a visitor waiting for him at the door, a part of him had secretly hoped Aubree had found her way there. Unfortunately, the sight of Max had not only killed the dream, it had the exact opposite reaction, especially once the bastard opened his mouth. He should've known agreeing to a DNA test would come back to bite him in his ass, but he could have never guessed how much.

"I want to know if you intend to see

my dad now since we know he was telling the truth."

Counting the passes, he moved back to his wrist from his knuckles while making sure he didn't lose any of the function in his hand. "No."

"What was the point in even agreeing to this test if you won't see him?"

"You wanted to know," Drew answered honestly. "Now, you do."

"What the fuck, man? Do you think I want to be doing this? Isn't it bad enough I have to listen to him rave over your success all the time? Now I have to come here and beg the guy who's fucking my girl to grant a dying man his wish."

Drew glanced over his shoulder at his mom. She kept her head bent over the paperwork sitting on her desk, but he knew she was listening to every word. He'd never been more thankful he'd already told her about Max, because the dude wasn't holding back. "You shouldn't let it bother you. I don't. Simply remind yourself how he was there for you every night, and never acknowledged my existence all these years. As far as Aubree goes, you shouldn't think too much about her either, since I can assure you she is not thinking of you."

With the tape secure, Drew had nothing else to distract him and was forced to meet Max's stare. "Is there anything else I can help you with?"

"Sure," Max said, his voice dripping with sarcasm. "You can back off Aubree."

"That's not happening."

Max's already thunderous frown turned darker at Drew's quick answer. "Is this some form of payback? You didn't have our dad so you steal something else from me?"

Drew shook his head feeling almost sorry for the guy. "I didn't steal anything from you. You had it all and threw it away. Damn man, Aubree is not a possession. She's a person with feelings, but you're too fucking selfish." Realizing his temper was slipping, he cut off the rant before he lost control. Counting to ten in his head, he said, "I'm so glad I agreed to find out if I'm related to you. Our family reunions will be oodles of fun. Now I have shit to do so, you know, don't let the door hit you in the ass on the way out."

There was a moment when Drew thought Max might hit him. The flash of pure hatred in his eyes told the whole story but with one last scathing look, he threw open the steel door. Drew didn't budge until it slammed closed behind Max, in case he chose to do something stupid. No Rival was Drew's club. It was the one place in the world where he didn't have to pretend to be the shining star. He hated that Max poisoned it. Praying for patience, he released his breath slowly. It wasn't enough. He scrubbed his hands over his head.

"Fuck!"

"Holy crap. He looks exactly like his father. It's uncanny," his mom said, reminding him of her presence.

He flashed an apologetic smile. "I'm sorry about this. I don't know why I thought agreeing to this test would be the end of things. I just..." He had no idea what he intended to say. He just wanted Max to go away. He just wanted to pretend he was conceived in vitro or some shit.

"Don't apologize to me about this ever again. You're a good person and you always do what's right, even when it's not easy. I'm the one who made all the wrong choices, but I'm not sorry either because those decisions gave me you. I will say this though—you need to watch out for that one. His head isn't in a good place and if his personality matches his dad's as much as his face does, then he's crazy."

* * * * *

Aubree's phone buzzed in the front pocket of her scrubs for the fifteenth time and she continued ignoring it. She'd checked the screen the first time, out of pure curiosity, but Max's name on the screen had killed any interest she had in answering it.

At the end of her twelve-hour shift, she gave into temptation. Slipping into the nearest restroom, she played the first message.

"Hey Aubree. The test results came back today." There was a pause and Max's already weary voice somehow managed to become even more so. "Yeah. So the DNA is a match and I guess I now have a brother. I wish you would talk to me. Let me explain." She cut off the rest of his message by hitting delete, moving on to the next missed call. This time, Drew's voice came through the line. "I'm sure you've already heard from Max." There was a long pause before he spoke again, but Aubree knew he was still there. "I thought I didn't care," he added and something about his voice caused a knot to form in her stomach. He cleared his throat. "Anyhow, call me when you get time."

Chewing on her lips, Aubree's mind raced in a thousand directions. She couldn't remember a time when she'd been so torn. Sliding her finger over the screen of her phone once more, she searched her contacts list. After a few well-placed calls and scribbling on her hand,

Aubree set out on foot. The address was little more than half a block away, and with the downtown traffic in full swing, she decided it would be quicker to walk.

Following the directions she'd been given, Aubree found the nondescript steel door inside a parking garage. She checked the numbers written on the back of her hand one last time before entering the passcode. The light above the security panel flashed green and Aubree tugged the door open. The smell drifting out of the open doorway almost made Aubree turn around and leave. She'd intentionally avoided the whole fight club scene since her parents' deaths, and the testosterone mixed with sweat hanging in the air brought a painful picture of their smiling faces to life.

Even though the sights and scents inside the building only brought back happy memories, it was a painful reminder of how alone she was now. Pushing the past aside, she concentrated on the present. There was an office right inside the door. Its plain concrete walls blocked a majority of the club from view. Peeking inside, she found it empty so she followed the sounds of voices and pounding blows until a few weight benches came into view. Unsure of how welcome her presence would be, she cast a worried glance around the low-lit interior, catching sight of a short, gray-haired woman who looked vaguely familiar. When the older woman turned in her direction, recognition slammed into Aubree and a bubble of happiness welled in her chest.

"Gigi!"

A radiant smile lit the woman's lips when Aubree called her name. Aubree rushed to her side. "Oh my goodness, Aubree. It's been such a long time." Throwing her arms around Gigi, Aubree hugged her father's longtime friend to her chest tightly. Gigi was four inches shorter than she was, and she'd gained a few pounds since Aubree had last seen her, but she still looked good for her age.

Gigi patted her gray hair as she pulled away as if checking to make sure Aubree hadn't messed it up. "How have you been?"

"I've been good," Aubree lied blatantly.

Gigi gave her forearm a comforting pat. "I'm guessing my boy called you with the news already." Aubree's eyebrows shot to her hairline at the woman's words. Gigi smiled knowingly as she added, "He hasn't stopped talking about you since the party."

A hint of worry over what exactly Drew had told his mother wormed its way through her, but she shook it off. Gesturing toward her scrubs, Aubree explained, "I was at work when I got his message, but I came straight over once my shift ended. Is he around?"

Gigi nodded toward a dark hallway to Aubree's left. "If you head down that way, you'll find him. He's in the middle of a sparring match, but it won't last long."

Aubree glanced at the passage feeling a bit nervous. A few men lingered around the nearby weights eyeing her curiously, and she wondered if she'd made a mistake coming here. Drew didn't seem as if he needed anyone. Gigi gave her a little shove from behind. "Go on." With a grateful smile, Aubree did as told. The farther she moved down the hall, the louder the echo of fists connecting with skin became. She'd seen several MMA fights in her lifetime and more than enough sparring matches. The sound of flesh meeting flesh was one people didn't easily forget. When the cage came into view, Aubree held her breath until she was positive it wasn't Drew who was taking the pounding.

She slowly released the air from her lungs when she caught sight of him. His face was set into a hard mask. A muscle ticked in Drew's jaw and a line of concentration pulled at his brows. Every well-defined muscle in his body seemed flexed and ready to attack as he circled his opponent on the mat. Aubree spared a quick glance for Drew's competitor noting he seemed fit as well, before returning to stare at Drew. In a move so quick, she almost missed it, Drew landed a blow to the other man's ribs before sweeping his feet out from beneath him. The other man went down but to Aubree's surprise, he let out a shout of laughter as he hit the mat.

"Good job, man. You're getting better at sneaking in the left-handed jab."

Drew chuckled as he helped the brown-haired man to his feet. As Drew clasped hands with his competitor, his gaze met hers. Drew said something she couldn't hear and the guy cast a glance in her direction. Grabbing a white towel from the edge of the mat, Drew headed toward her. His expression gave away nothing and she wondered again if she'd made a mistake. As he cleared the door of the cage, he swiped the towel down the front of his sculpted body. Aubree followed the motion with her eyes. The flat pads of his chest flared into wide shoulders. He tossed the towel aside a few feet away from her and Aubree stared at his stomach.

Every built man Aubree had ever encountered sported a six-pack, but Drew had a super sexy eight-pack. The hint of a tattoo peeked out at the edge of his shorts, and she tore her eyes away from the sight in fear she would push the material aside to learn what it said.

"I got your message," she said, explaining her presence. Without another thought, she met him halfway, walking straight into his embrace. The fine sheen of sweat covering his body clung to her clothes as he closed his arms around her.

Resting his chin on her head, he spoke into her hair. "I'm glad you're here."

Aubree closed her eyes as she pressed her ear to his chest. "I came as soon as my shift ended."

His arms tightened around her waist. "That explains the sexy cartoon characters on your scrubs." He chuckled when she huffed and held her in place when she made a halfhearted attempt to pull away. Keeping hold of her waist, he leaned back enough to see her face, and despite his laughter, his face was unnaturally serious. "It means more to me than you realize. Am I allowed to keep you for a little while or do you have other plans?"

*

She could have as easily chosen to go to Max. Drew had beaten back the reality of things the entire day. Aubree had been friends with Max longer. In spite of the things the man had done, Drew knew she might still go to him. Even as he held her to his chest, he still couldn't believe she hadn't. He fought back his natural urge to overcome her, bending her to his will as he awaited her answer.

"I need a shower, but otherwise I'm

yours for the evening."

"I need a shower too."

Aubree laughed but made no move to pull away. "Really? I hadn't noticed."

"This is nothing. Imagine how much sweat there will be when I finally have my way with you."

"Ah," Aubree sighed. "There's the Drew I know and love."

Although he knew she didn't mean the words, they still hung in the air between them. Without giving her a chance to guess at his intentions, he dipped his head and touched his lips to hers. It wasn't really a kiss, merely a promise of things to come. He pulled away before she could protest. "You don't get to take it back," he said, knowing she would understand what he meant. Stepping away, he added, "If you don't mind hanging out for a few minutes, I'll jump in

the shower here and then take you home.
I'm in the mood to pamper you."

Without waiting for her response, he
strolled away. It wasn't until he was in the
shower that he realized there was nothing
keeping her from leaving. She'd found her
way there and she could as easily find her
way out again. Once the idea settled into
his mind, he couldn't get done with his
shower fast enough. Rushing through the
motions, he threw on an old pair of jeans
and t-shirt without bothering to dry off.
Since he kept his head shaved, hair wasn't
an issue for him. It was the annoyance of
struggling to pull a pair of jeans over
soaking wet skin that had him in a panic.

His anxiety didn't subside until he
caught a flash of her blonde hair inside the
front office. Even then, he didn't draw
another easy breath until he saw her face.
Deep in conversation with his mother,

Aubree didn't notice him right away. He stole a moment of simply watching her. Drew found it almost funny how oblivious Aubree was to her effect on men. They all stopped to watch her when she walked into a room. It wasn't just her gorgeous body or beautiful eyes. In fact, there wasn't anything about her that wasn't sexy as hell, but Aubree also glowed from the inside. It took one glance in her direction and men were hooked.

His mother smiled at him knowingly, but Drew couldn't dredge up an ounce of shame over her catching him ogling Aubree. Obviously sensing something going on, Aubree turned in her seat and the same feeling that had overcome him the first time he'd seen her happened all over again at her open happiness at seeing him.

"Are you ready?" At his question,

both women came to their feet, and Aubree gave his mother a quick hug before moving to his side.

"It was nice to see you again. I hope we can get together soon," Aubree told his mother, and he could tell she meant her words. After a quick exchange of pleasantries, Drew motioned Aubree through the door. His mother snagged his arm. Hissing under her breath, she made sure Aubree couldn't hear her. "Love her! Do not let this one get away."

"Not gonna happen," he said without hesitation. He knew Aubree was still struggling against the truth, but sooner or later, she would to have to accept her fate. She belonged to him.

This time as he drove Aubree home, she was a bit more animated. She began with a story about another nurse she worked with, from there moved into the patients she dealt with each day. It was obvious from the tone of her voice, she loved her job, and she possessed an uncanny ability to find the humor in every situation.

It wasn't until he'd followed her all the way into her bedroom that she seemed to realize she'd not stopped talking the whole time. A blush touched her cheeks. "I'm so sorry. I swear I'll be quiet now and let you have a turn."

"I've got nothing," he admitted. "I have a match coming up so I haven't done anything but train lately."

"Oh a match. See you did have something."

"Come with me. You'll be right up front."

Her mouth lifted in one corner, and a mischievous glint entered her eyes. "Are you asking me on a date?"

"I guess I am. Does it matter? You've already managed to charm me all the way into your bedroom."

Aubree glanced around as if only now realizing where they were standing. "Wow. I am good." In spite of the teasing note to her voice, she shifted nervously from foot to foot and he immediately regretted pointing out their surroundings.

"Go take your shower," he said, urging her on. "I'll be right here waiting on you." To punctuate his statement, he toed off his shoes, and leapt onto her bed. It was considerably softer than he anticipated and he sank in about two inches upon impact. "Holy hell. This mattress is awesome," he said as he climbed up to the head of the king-sized bed and settled back onto the pillows.

"You have a knack for making yourself at home."

"I've been in your bed. You'll never get rid of me now." As he said the words, the mattress conformed to his body, and he leaned over the edge to pull up the sheet to get a closer look. "Shit. I'm really not joking. What the hell is this thing made out of?"

"It's some type of foam," she explained as she moved to the dresser and pulled out some clothes.

"Whatever it is, I'm already addicted, and you're stuck with me."

"See what you're missing out on by living in a hotel?" Without waiting for his response, she moved to the closet and came out with a towel. "I'll be right back," she added as she headed for the bathroom attached to her bedroom.

"Do you need any help? I might have missed a few spots myself when I showered earlier."

She growled as she slammed the bathroom door and he couldn't help but laugh. He knew she thought he was outrageous, but what she didn't realize was, it was her. He was normally a somber person, but when he was with her, things popped out of his mouth without his permission. Snagging another pillow, he crammed it under his head before settling back down again. The bed met him halfway. "Fucking hell," he moaned in memory foam heaven. "I'm going to have to marry her."

Aubree's bedroom was the least girly room in her apartment. The dresser, bedside table and entertainment center were all solid oak while her comforter was some crazy dark abstract thing he couldn't seem to look away from. It wasn't bad though, he mused in a valiant attempt to distract himself from what was taking place on the other side of the closed door. With every splash of water, he imagined her hands sliding over her body and he had to fight the urge to kick the door in. The bathroom didn't seem very big from the outside, which meant the shower was probably small, but he wouldn't need much room to bring her pleasure.

With his dick begging for release and his mind completely in the gutter, Drew cast a glance around the room in hopes of finding anything else to concentrate on. In his desperate bid for distraction, he made the biggest mistake of all. He slid open the drawer of the table beside him. Although he hadn't thought such a thing possible, his shaft hardened even more, and he quickly closed the drawer. Draping his arm over his eyes to shut out the room, he concentrated on bringing his body under control. He'd known Aubree wasn't a puritan, and he was damn glad for it, but he'd still been surprised by the collection of toys. The water shut off and he begged his dick to cooperate. He would have her. It was only a matter of time. When it happened, he'd make sure she became so addicted to his touch, she'd never shake him. However, today wasn't the day. She wasn't ready for him yet.

The bathroom door opened and he turned on his side grabbing a handful of comforter along the way. He managed to hide his erection from sight while exposing the sheets next to him. He patted the spot beside him. "I'm not getting out of this awesome bed so you'll have to join me."

She'd twisted her hair into a clip at the crown of her head and changed into a pair of yoga pants and a cotton form-fitting shirt. He knew she wasn't trying to tempt him, but she still was, and he ground his back teeth to keep from pouncing on her. Thankfully, instead of the argument he was expecting, she climbed onto the bed and settled in next to him. At the last second, he pulled one of his knees up to keep her from pressing too close, and to his amazement, she simply threw her legs over his and scooted in until her shoulder hit his chest. Incapable of resisting her, he slipped his arm beneath her head.

The delicious smell rolling off her body did nothing to ease his lust. As she stared silently at the ceiling, he contemplated what she would sound like as she came against his mouth. As he wondered if he would start panting soon, she asked, "Why me?"

With his brain no longer fully functioning, he couldn't process her question. "Why you what?"

She turned her head, meeting his stare. "I imagine you know thousands of people," she explained. "But you're here with me. Why?"

Of all the topics she could've chosen to discuss, she landed on the one that immediately brought his body back in check. "I don't know anyone," he admitted. "Everyone I know is a fake. Everyone I meet lies to me and tells me what I want to hear." He hated to say the man's name and bring him between them, but Drew needed to make her understand. "Take Ryan as the perfect example. I met him while he was going from club to club, asking if he could leave brochures for his self-defense classes. He struck up a conversation with me and even as I recognized he was after something, I didn't guard myself against it. I thought he was angling for the free weekend at the casino, which he ended up with. Obviously, I could've never guessed his true intentions, but still, it's always the same with everyone I meet. Most of the time, I don't care because I'm fairly self-sufficient, but today when I got the news about Max, it mattered. You're not like anyone else. Not once have I felt as if you want anything from me."

Her expression never changed as he made his confession. He was grateful she didn't show him an ounce of pity. He really didn't need it. He had more money than most people in the world and he was well aware of it. But when it came to Aubree, it mattered.

After a moment, Aubree said, "I am after something from you. Your friendship and your time are something I've come to realize I want more than anything." His heart swelled at her words, but she wasn't finished. "I also yearn to bask in your wildly inappropriate remarks. You make me a bit uncomfortable with your overwhelming presence and I crave it. Come to think of it, I probably expect more from you than anyone you've ever met."

Clearing his throat, Drew did his best to talk in spite of feeling as if someone were sitting on his chest. "I expect some things in return."

Aubree gave him a solemn nod as if she would accept no less. "Go on."

Keeping a straight face, he ran down his list, "Your undying love and affection along with your unwavering loyalty." Aubree covered her face with her hands and let out a snort of laughter, but he didn't let up. "I also demand sexual favors and at least half this bed, which I suspect was actually handcrafted by fairies."

"Oh shut up!" she cried, playfully slapping at his shoulder. He caught her hand, holding it in place.

"Okay, I'm being serious now," he said, making sure he had her full attention before adding, "I want as much of you as you're willing to give. Your friendship means more to me than I can explain, but I'm not joking about the sexual favors. I'm really going to do some naughty things to you."

"For the love of..." Aubree sighed, giving in. "Tell me about your upcoming match. Who is your opponent, and what are your chances of winning? Is he hot?"

His cheeks hurt from smiling. Drew refused to let her bait him. Instead, he bored her to tears with training strategies and fighting stats. She looked completely wiped out.

The longer he spoke the more he

intentionally dropped the pitch of his voice, lulling her to sleep. Spending time with her was enough. He didn't need her to keep him entertained. He let her doze for close to an hour while he simply enjoyed watching every nuance of her face while completely unguarded. Aubree slept with her chin tilted toward him, and she curled against him so trustingly. He couldn't look away. Drew traced the curve of her cheek with his eyes until—giving in to temptation—he cupped her face in his hand. She snuggled closer to his chest at his touch. Everything he felt and every intention he had toward her became clear. Being with her had nothing to do with besting anyone, as Max accused. She wasn't a game to him. While it was true, he couldn't pretend as if he hadn't seen the way Ryan and Max looked at her, even before he'd known the truth of their relationship, it wasn't about stealing her away from them. Drew cared about her more than he had anyone in a long time. A few short minutes after meeting her, she'd managed to make him want to fight for her.

With his fingers splayed across her cheek, he brushed his thumb along her bottom lip as he urged her closer. Settling his lips at the corner of her mouth, he inhaled the scent of her skin into his lungs before opening his mouth over her bottom lip and sucking it between his teeth. His stomach growled as the tang of cherries exploded across his taste buds. The weight of her hand fell across the nape of his neck and she stroked his tongue with her own. He knew she was more asleep than awake. He didn't have any intention of dragging her from her dreams. It was the driving need to experience this moment with her causing him to act. With an internal cry of denial, he untangled himself from her hold and whispered against her ear. "Go back to sleep. I didn't mean to wake you."

Doing as he bade, she turned on her side. He hauled her against his chest. Even as he swore he'd never be able to sleep with her hips cradled by his, the darkness pulled him under.

*

Aubree jerked awake. She immediately reached for Drew, finding him gone. The smell of his cologne lingered, proving he hadn't been a dream. She cursed her stupidity as her heart ached over the loss of his warmth. One day, she swore she'd stop longing for things she couldn't have. Tears sprang to Aubree's eyes, adding to her annoyance with herself. Funnily enough, she'd never realized she was weak until recently. The discovery wasn't a pleasant one. With a groan, Aubree slapped her forehead. She was a pathetic chick with no way to work since her car was still at the hospital.

"Idiot," she grumbled, throwing the covers back. Swinging her legs over the side of the bed, she caught sight of a note leaning against the lamp on her bedside table. She pressed her lips together in a vain attempt to suppress a smile. *Weak,* she reminded herself harshly as she reached for the paper. Drew's handwriting was as bold as the rest of him, Aubree realized as she read the words in front of her.

Your car is out front. I'll see you tonight—D.

Aubree jumped from the bed, rushed to the window, and peeked out. Sure enough, her car was sitting at the curb. She didn't know how Drew had pulled it off, but somehow he always managed perfection. Brushing her fingertips over her lips, she pictured his kiss. She'd been half-awake, but she knew it hadn't been a dream. A nervous flutter started in the pit of her stomach. The soft, undemanding way his mouth had settled over hers ran through her mind once more. It was official. She was fucked. Whereas Ryan and Max had stung her pride with their betrayal, Drew would burn her life to the ground if he didn't return, except he did.

Every night after the first one he spent sleeping at her side, Drew continued turning up at her door. Sometimes she would find him waiting on her porch. He always carefully avoided her questions on how long he'd been there. Finally, she worried over it so much, she gave him a key. His triumphant smile told her how easily she'd been maneuvered. Secretly she wondered who'd lured whom into the other's constant company. Aubree couldn't get enough of his scandalous sense of humor and hot glances, but the bite of reality kept her from acting on her desires. She'd proven how stupid she could truly be already.

Chapter Six

The fight Drew trained endlessly for rolled in like a freight train. Aubree wasn't prepared. It was facing two fears at once for her. She had to choke down the memories of the times she spent going to these events with her father, accepting he was gone, while witnessing Drew under attack. Pushing those things aside, Aubree concentrated on Drew and refused to show him how she was really feeling. His room in the back was a private one, but the sound of the crowd still filled the tiny space reverberating from the walls. Gigi hovered in the doorway waiting for Aubree to say her goodbyes.

"Mom knows where your seat is located. She won't let you get lost in the mayhem."

"Don't worry over me," she fussed. Drew leaned in, touching his forehead to hers.

She stared into eyes, determined to be the best damn cheer section he'd ever had.

An official poked his head in over Gigi's shoulder. "It's time to get your tape signed off on."

"You'll win," Aubree reassured him.

Drew flashed a confident smile. "I know." With a crook of his finger, he called her closer and spoke against her ear. "I feel it's only fair to warn you, before the end of this night, I'll be inside you and you'll never be able have another orgasm without thinking of me."

Heat exploded across Aubree's face and Drew threw his head back, laughing. Punctuating his promise, he touched his lips to hers quickly. "Now go with Mom. I

146

want to know where you are."

Pulling away, Aubree did as he bade and followed Gigi through the packed aisles until they made their way to the edge of the steel cage. Finding their seats, Aubree sucked in a deep breath as she sat down, doing her best not to think about anything. It was hard work making her mind a blank slate.

Gigi patted her knee. "Sweetie, you won't have time to worry."

It wasn't exactly the truth. Aubree had to sit through two matches before Drew's, and she chewed on her nails while counting blows. Some lessons she'd not forgotten over the years, it seemed, since she knew the exact moment both matches were over, and who won when it came down to scoring hits. By the time Drew's name was announced, Aubree thought she'd be sick. The roar inside the building was deafening when he entered the cage. His opponent seemed pumped and fit, adding to her nervousness. She knew Drew would win, but she didn't want him to so much as get hit. While the names were being called and the rules read, Drew moved to the wire where she sat, linking his fingers through. He stared at her without saying a word, but she could feel the intensity rolling off him in waves. He was in battle mode but still there in the moment with her. The look was so hot she fanned her face. When he broke their connection, it felt almost physical.

"Wow," Gigi said, causing Aubree to blush.

Drawn back into reality by the sound of the bell, her stomach fell when Drew's opponent proved to be every bit as quick as he appeared, landing a solid kick to Drew's ribs. The sound echoed in her ears but Drew never flinched. Taking advantage of the man's need to reset his balance after the move, Drew struck. His fist connected solidly with the guy's chin and he went down hard. Aubree blinked owlishly as her mind attempted to accept it was already over. As the judge called it, Drew walked back to the cage where she sat and knocked his fist against the steel twice, before placing his hand over his heart. Keeping his eyes locked on her, he raised his arms in victory and walked backward toward the judge.

Gigi bumped Aubree's shoulder, dragging her out of her haze. "You're the one."

"What?" Aubree asked in confusion.

"For my son," Gigi clarified. "Everybody only gets one, you know, and you're the one for Drew."

Without thinking, Aubree scoffed.

"Drew's probably met a thousand of the perfect one." Realizing not only what she'd said but to whom she'd said it, Aubree groaned in mortification, but Gigi chuckled.

"I'm not exaggerating. You don't realize it, but my son is easily the most serious man on the planet. He doesn't joke, tease or laugh." After a moment, she added, "Actually, he doesn't even talk very much, come to think of it, but he does all those things when you're around. Look at him right now."

Aubree did as Gigi bade. Drew stood in the center of the mat shaking hands and nodding as people spoke. His face was a hardened mask. There was none of the humor in him she'd become accustomed to seeing. She was watching a stranger. Gigi leaned closer. "That is my son. He is wonderful but also an impenetrable island."

Aubree continued studying him in wonder until—almost as if he felt her regard—Drew turned his head, meeting her gaze. A mischievous grin passed over his lips and she knew he was thinking of his earlier promise.

"And there is the Drew he's become since meeting you," Gigi said, sounding satisfied over making her point.

The ride home was a silent one as Aubree continued mulling over Gigi's words. Drew was such an overwhelming force of nature, she'd never considered he wasn't the same person twenty-four hours a day. There wasn't anything special about her. She didn't have anything to offer someone like him, but she also could not deny what she'd seen with her own eyes. Testing a theory, she turned her head enough to bring him into her line of sight.

The lights from the dashboard cast enough glow for her to see his face was completely devoid of emotion as he concentrated on the road in front of them. Testing a theory, she reached across the darkened car, touching his arm. The moment her skin connected with his, Drew's face transformed and he let go of the wheel. Linking his fingers with hers, he brought her hand to his lips. The tip of his tongue touched her knuckles. Her body went haywire at the small caress. When he did it a second time, she nearly whimpered as her pussy clenched. Tugging her an inch closer, he repeated the action on the inside of her wrist. This time, she couldn't stop the sound from escaping.

They made it to her house and Drew had her out of the car with her back pressed against her front door before she realized what was happening. His wide shoulders protected her from the view of any passing motorist as he settled his lips over hers. It was total consumption. There was no other way Aubree could explain the way he kissed her. She swore she could taste his lust, and pride roared through her with the knowledge a man such as Drew wanted her. He'd said the words, but people lied and flirted all the time without really meaning it. His touch was the most honest thing she'd ever encountered. He was using every weapon in his arsenal against her. His tongue, teeth and even the vibration of his voice as he encouraged her to go farther with every passing second, combined with the way he touched her, stealing her sense. With one hand buried in her hair and one gripping her ass, he kept her pinned in place. When he pulled away, she could barely breathe.

She could feel his heart racing beneath her fingertips, but his breathing held steady. Keeping her gaze locked on his mouth, her heart skipped a beat. The world went dark around the edges as her vision narrowed to a pinpoint. Everything became crystal clear in her mind. He was a perfect mixture of Max and Ryan. She'd never been able to choose between the two men because together they possessed all the qualities she searched for in one man. Drew had it all. He could be intense and serious, smiles and happiness. He was dark and light with single-minded focus, which would leave her sated. He watched her with hooded eyes, and the words fell from her lips before she could stop them.

"I don't know what to do."

His mouth lifted in one corner and she stared at his bottom lip, swollen from her kisses, in fascination. "Yes you do."

"I do?"

"Yes. You want to invite me inside so I can show you what it would be like if you chose to keep me."

She couldn't stop the question. "Do you want to be kept?"

"I'm fighting my nature here as we speak. I want to throw you over my shoulder and steal you away from this place. I want to hide you away while I show you every pleasure your body is capable of enduring. I don't intend to let you come up for air until I've touched, tasted, explored and penetrated until you've accepted you are mine."

An image of Drew doing all the things he mentioned flashed across her mind. A shiver of yearning ran through her as moisture flooded her core. His nostrils flared, as if he could smell her lust. His hold tightened on her waist. She licked her suddenly parched lips, and let her head fall back against the door. "I hate wanting you so much," she admitted. "I have this burning desire to believe everything you say to me, but I don't know how. It's not as if I think you're dishonest. I can't trust myself anymore."

"You cared about Ryan and Max because you were friends. Yes, it included benefits, but in the end, you weren't upset by the outcome. That says more than you realize. Maybe you're angry over the secrets they kept from you and the loss of their companionship but make no mistake, you are mine. You can keep fighting and I will keep chasing you, but in the end, the result will be the same. It will be my name you're moaning."

She stared speechless at his mouth. It was true. She couldn't deny a thing he said. She wanted to give in and he knew it. Gripping the door frame, he boxed her in with his arms. "Do you need me to demand it and set you free from guilt?" She remained stubbornly silent. "Open the door, Aubree. You once told me you expect more from me than anyone else ever has. I'm calling you on it now. Take me inside and give me the entire list." At his commanding tone, she did as he bade. He followed her inside, closing the door behind them. The lock clicking in place sounded unnaturally loud in the quiet house.

Drew made no move to touch her. Instead, he crossed his arms over his chest and leaned his back against the inside of the door. "I'm wait—"

"Take your clothes off," Aubree said interrupting him.

*

Aubree was easily the most "both feet in"

person he'd ever met. Once she made up her mind, she pushed doubt aside and he could see it written all over her face. This wasn't her merely giving in. She would challenge him to meet every boast he'd made. Straightening away from the door, Drew watched her closely as he pulled his shirt over his head and tossed it aside. Prowling toward her, he waited until the last second before veering to the right and sitting on the edge of the couch. In the otherwise silent house, he heard her indrawn breath. He kept his smile hidden as he untied his work boots. Slipping them from his feet, he shoved them beneath the coffee table. As he stood once more, he pulled his leather belt loose. Her eyes followed every move his hands made. His cock reacted as if she boldly stroked it when he pushed his jeans past his hips baring the rest of his body. She stepped closer.

"I've been dying to know," Aubree said, brushing her fingertips along his hip. She sat on the coffee table, forcing him to turn in her direction. Staring at the top of her head in a position he'd fantasized about more than once caused his dick to weep. A drop of semen leaked from the tip. Instead of doing what he hoped, she traced the lines of the word *Unsurpassed*, which was tattooed between his navel and hip. "I've caught flashes of it several times and it's been killing me to know what it was."

Brushing her hair aside, he traced the line of her cheek. "All you had to do was ask."

Ignoring his words, she trailed her fingers over his "v" muscle. "I'm never sure what this spot right here is actually called, but it makes me want to do this." Leaning forward, she opened her mouth over the place she'd pointed out. Something in his jaw popped as he called on every ounce of his control.

Panting, he answered her question. "It's an oblique. You're a nurse. You should know this shit." She chuckled as she followed the line of muscle with her tongue until she was half an inch away from his shaft. "You're a cruel woman."

Aubree tilted her chin back meeting his eyes. The look of unadulterated lust on her face almost broke him. He'd never been so tested in his life. "I thought you expected a list of things I want from you."

"I do."

She buried her nails into the back of his thighs and urged him forward. "I want you to let me have my way," she said, as she took him between her lips. His self-control lasted long enough for Aubree to tighten her throat around his cock one time. Snatching her from the table, he lifted her over his shoulder and strode toward the bedroom.

"Next time," he promised. She roared with laughter as he tossed her onto the bed and peeled off her clothes. She tried to help but he pushed her hands aside. He'd been fantasizing about this moment and he wouldn't miss it. The moment he had her divested of her clothing, Drew froze, standing over her, almost mesmerized by the sight of her bare skin.

"You're fucking amazing. I think I owe my mom a thank-you card for the extra ten pounds you definitely do not need to lose."

Aubree snorted. "This might not be the best time to talk about your mom."

Releasing a deep chuckle, Drew slid open the drawer of the nightstand and pulled out a handful of condoms. Aubree's eyebrows lifted. "I don't recall having those."

Drew tossed all but one on top of the stand as he taunted her. "I have my ways." He tore at the plastic with his teeth and Aubree sat up, letting her legs dangle over the edge of the bed. She took the condom from him and slowly rolled it down his shaft as if determined to make him insane. He could tell by her impish smile she was enjoying his torment a bit too much.

"Enough," he said, stepping out of her hold. "It's my turn." He went over to the dresser, found a pair of silk panties and returned to Aubree's side.

"Up," he ordered, pointing toward the headboard until Aubree obeyed. Climbing onto the mattress, Drew straddled her hips pinning her in place. "Do you trust me?" At her nod, a shout of satisfaction rang through his head. He ran his hands up her body forcing her arms above her head. "Hang onto the headboard, baby, and don't let go."

Aubree wrapped her fingers around one of the oak rungs without question. He twisted the material around her wrist before securing her hands to the wood. She could easily escape the knot, but he hoped she would play along. Her eyes were slightly unfocused and her nipples were hardened into tiny beads. The picture of feminine lust she painted was every man's dream.

"I've spent every night since we met wondering what you sound like when you come." Dipping his head, he sucked her nipple into his mouth, flattening his tongue over it once before pulling away again and adding, "Let's find out."

Shifting positions until he was on

his knees with her open thighs draped across his, Drew traced the seam of her cunt with the tips of his fingers before spreading her pussy lips wide. Aubree was dripping. She whimpered as he pressed two fingers inside coating them with her juices. A growl rose in his throat when her warm channel squeezed the digits.

"Damn, you're tight. I need you relaxed and ready if you're going to accept me."

"Ready now," she gasped out causing him to bite back an evil grin.

"No," he argued, using her moisture to circle her clit. "You're still fighting me and trying to anticipate my next move." Without warning, he pushed past the tight ring of muscles in her ass. She moaned and writhed at the intrusion. "You're so fucking responsive. It makes me want to try a thousand things at once."

Drew was feigning a patience he didn't truly possess. His dick beat a drum pattern against his navel and he could feel the blood pounding through it. The force of Aubree's reactions to his caress made him want to drag out the experience. He couldn't get enough. It was addicting.

"Please, Drew?"

His eyes fell closed as he savored the sound of his name falling from her lips in the perfect tone of sexual need. Reluctantly, he pulled away. Leaning past her, he dug around in the bedside table once more. This time, he came back with a few toys.

"I won't leave you unsatisfied," he promised.

He didn't ask for her preference before slipping the anal plug inside her. Aubree's hips left the bed, but he wasn't done. Spreading her lips wide once more, he exposed the tiny bud hidden from sight. After turning the vibrator to its highest speed, he pressed it against her. The muscles in his stomach clenched in anticipation as she moved her hips in time with his strokes, taking her pleasure from him. She threw her head back and gasped as the first spasm hit. Drew couldn't wait any longer. Tossing the toy aside, he buried his cock inside her while her channel continued pulsing, allowing her pussy to milk him. A sound he could only describe as carnal tore from her throat and he swallowed it down, shoving his tongue into her mouth. She sucked on it greedily as he rocked against her, making sure to grind down on her clit with each stroke.

It seemed no sooner had one spasm ended than a second round began, taking Drew by surprise with the power of her muscles constricting around his shaft. Aubree sank her teeth into his bottom lip, and his balls drew up in expectation of release. Something shifted inside his chest as the hot jet of semen shot from the head of Drew's cock. His body was nothing more than a mass of nerve endings focused solely on the sensation of possessing Aubree. Even after the explosion passed, he couldn't shake the feeling.

Her ragged breaths fanned across his cheek and her pebbled nipples brushed his chest. Her inner thighs pressed against his hips as she cradled him with her body. Tiny aftershock pulsations continued tugging at his shaft. He was more than aware of every place she touched him. Pressing a kiss to her jawline, he reluctantly pulled out. Her hips followed him as if she fought to hang onto him. "Don't worry. I'm not done with you," he whispered against her skin before pushing away from the mattress and heading for the bathroom. He needed to get them both cleaned up, but Drew meant every word he said. Aubree Holiday had sealed her fate by allowing him inside her. Now he'd never be done.

*

Aubree lingered somewhere between awake and dreaming as she rested in the cradle of Drew's arms. She didn't know how long she'd been dozing off and on before his voice cut through the dark.

"You're unlike any woman I've ever met before."

The silence stretched on as she waited for Drew to say more. When he didn't, she asked, "How so?"

Coming up onto his elbow, he leaned over her. Realizing sleep was lost to her, Aubree stared up at him as he brushed his knuckles along her jaw. Drew's eyes followed the motion with a tenderness she'd never believed possible.

"You have bursts of extreme animation but for the most part, you're almost always quiet," he explained. "Except for your eyes." His gaze moved to hers and she was ensnared. "Sometimes they have so much to say, I can't look away. I feel as if we have entire conversations without speaking a word."

It was true. She felt the same, and she found herself admitting her secrets. "I'm always begging you to touch me in my mind and hoping you'll see it when I look at you."

"You're amazing," he said, brushing his thumb over her bottom lip before reaching down to swipe the covers from her nude body. Without warning, he cupped her mound. "And I can't seem to stop wanting you," he added as he stroked her inflamed flesh. Finding her tender nub, Drew rolled it between his thumb and forefinger drawing a moan from deep inside her. Her focus turned inward as she concentrated on the tingling of her pussy.

She groaned in protest when he withdrew his touch and licked his fingers. His eyes fell closed as he seemed to savor her taste. When they opened again, heat radiated from his stare. "First, I'll fuck you with my tongue," he warned. "And once you're screaming my name, I intend to slip my dick inside your tight pussy and ride out the waves." She was on the verge of orgasm with his words alone.

Dipping his head, he closed his mouth over her nipple and Aubree whimpered in her need as his rough tongue pulled at the hardened point. Clutching his head to her chest, Aubree closed her eyes and gave herself over to the moment. Every place his lips touched seemed to have a direct line to her pussy. By the time he stroked his tongue over her clit she was primed for release. Digging her nails into Drew's shoulders, she gasped as stars exploded behind her eyelids. He moaned and the sound sent vibrations through her. She pushed closer to his tongue, riding out the waves.

Crawling up her body, Drew reached over snagging a condom from the bedside table. While holding her gaze, he ripped the gold package open with his teeth. Aubree enjoyed every second of the show as he donned it. By the time the blunt head of his cock was pressing against her entrance, she was begging for it.

"Hurry. I want to feel all of you."

His lips settled over hers as he

pushed his way inside and Aubree sucked in a sharp breath. All her longing came to the surface. She bit down hard on the delicious bottom lip that constantly teased her with its wickedness. He was perfect. There was no way she'd get to keep him. As the champion, he could have any woman he chose. For tonight, he belonged to her. If this was the only night she'd have with Drew, she wanted to taste as much of him as possible. Aubree was so wet she could hear it with every pump of his hips. Ripping his mouth away, Drew buried his face against her neck.

"Fuck, Aubree. You have to come for me. I want to feel your greedy cunt pulling at my cock. Come for me, now."

Punctuating his words by reaching between them and circling her tender nub, Drew sent her over the edge again. With her focus on the tingling and pulsing of her pussy, she barely noticed the tightening of his muscles as his body tensed. Drew cursed heavily when his orgasm hit. He crushed her beneath him. Aubree could barely breathe underneath his full weight. She didn't care. She memorized every dip and valley of his back as she ran her hands over his skin. He was so much more than every fantasy she'd ever had, and this was one she wanted to keep.

Chapter Seven

"Ho! Ho! Ho!" Aubree turned her head, hiding her smile from the tiny girl in the hospital bed as Drew entered the room. Despite keeping her gaze locked on the white dry erase board in front of her, he could tell from the outline of her cheek she was holding back laughter.

She quickly finished writing a series of numbers on the board and seemed to have pulled herself together by the time she turned around. Her eyes shone as she cheered, "It's Santa! He's made a special trip to see you, Trina."

The little girl hid a shy smile as Drew claimed the chair next to her bed. The stuffing at his stomach took some getting used to, and the fake beard was hot as hell, but the smile on the kids' faces had been worth it.

"I'll leave the two of you alone, but I expect you to ask for something expensive since Santa can afford it." Drew bit back a laugh at Aubree's words. She winked as she left the room.

"How are you today?" Drew asked as soon as they were alone. Trina's advance-stage cancer had left her little more than skin over bones and chemo had stolen her hair. In spite of those things, she seemed strong, if not a little old for her ten years.

She ran her finger underneath the plastic ID bracelet on her arm, keeping her eyes locked on the motion as she answered. "I'm okay."

"Your nurse, Aubree, tells me you've been very good this year, so I made a trip to see you. Do you have a special request?"

She kept up the nervous motion at her wrist. "I know you're not really Santa."

This was different. "What makes you say so?" Drew asked, hoping he didn't spoil Christmas for Trina for the rest of her life.

"It's Christmas Eve, so Santa is really busy, and that's why he sends his helpers out to talk to the kids." Luckily, she didn't appear to need his confirmation on the matter, before asking, "Do I have to ask for something for me?"

"Hmm, I don't suppose so, but don't you want a present for yourself?"

Trina curled her nose as if thinking things over. "I'm not really allowed to have many toys here since they absorb germs." Her answer broke Drew's heart. Kids should have toys, and it was a shame Trina had to accept that she couldn't. "But it's okay because I know what I want," she added sounding pragmatic.

"Hit me with your list."

"It's not for me," she reminded him.

Smiling at her motherly tone, he reassured her. "I'll do my best."

"I'd like for Aubree to get some happiness for Christmas." Drew's heart stopped at Trina's request. "Aubree isn't happy?"

"She is for part of the day," Trina explained. "I think she should be happy all day. She is very nice and I don't like that man who is mean to her."

"There's a man who's mean to her?" Drew heard himself, but he couldn't stop. If something was going on with Aubree, he needed to know, even if it meant questioning a child. Trina nodded while staring at the corner. "Un-huh. He shows up every day. He's very big," she explained holding her arms out wide to aid her description. "And he says lots of bad words to her. He says she only cares about sick kids and not sick old people then he calls her ugly names. I don't like him, and it's not true. Aubree cares about everybody, even the mean nurse who doesn't let me watch anything except the educational channel."

Drew gripped the arms of the chair until his knuckles protested. "Does he do anything else?" Even to his ears, Drew's voice sounded hollow.

Trina went back to twisting her bracelet. "Yesterday she said something and he got really mad. Aubree doesn't know I can see her from here with the door open," Trina added shooting him a panicked look.

"Don't worry," he said attempting to sound soothing in spite of his boiling blood. "I won't say a word. What happened yesterday?"

Looking relieved, Trina dropped her

gaze to her lap again. "He said, 'if you ask him to do it, he will. He'll give you whatever you want,' and Aubree told him no. She said, 'Everyone uses Drew. I love him and I won't be like everyone else.' His face turned scary and he pushed her against the wall. It was really hard too because she hit her head."

The edges of the room turned dark as Drew lost focus. He would kill him. Max had been here terrorizing Aubree and she hadn't said a word. He'd put his hands on her. Max was a dead man. "If he goes away, Aubree will smile again all day. Can you do it or am I wasting my Christmas wish?"

Every single word Trina spoke sounded as if it was coming through a tunnel, but he nodded. "I definitely can," he promised, and Trina looked over at him, smiling. Clenching both arms of the chair to keep from storming out, Drew forced his voice to remain level. "Are you sure there's nothing I can bring you for Christmas? I'll take care of Aubree for free if you'd like something as well."

She scrunched up her face again as she answered. "If you want to surprise me then I won't complain about whatever you bring me."

"You have a deal," he said, coming to his feet. He tried hard to move as slowly as possible even as his mind raced in every direction.

"It's okay for you to hug me."

In spite of his rage, Drew couldn't help but be charmed by the little girl as he leaned over and carefully hugged her. He was hyper-aware of his strength in comparison to her frail body, but it was obvious she had enough inner strength to make up the difference.

With a final wave, he headed out. As soon as he was out of sight, he stormed from the building pulling off the hat and beard as he went. It was time to take care of Max. Nobody touched his woman and lived to tell about it.

*

Aubree peeked in Trina's room and a hint of disappointment set in when she realized she'd missed saying goodbye to Drew. "I see Santa has already left."

Trina nodded. "He is Santa, so he's very busy today."

Aubree pursed her lips to keep from smiling at Trina's matter-of-fact tone. She was convinced the girl would grow to be quite the character. "Did you make sure to ask for lots of new stuff?"

"He's going to surprise me."

"Good choice," Aubree agreed. "I like surprises." Glancing over she caught sight of the television. "Sheesh. Are you on the educational channel again? Be a child, chickee," Aubree ordered flipping it to the cartoon channel as Trina giggled.

Despite her best efforts, Aubree spent the rest of the day worrying. Even though she knew Drew had a lot to do, it wasn't like him to leave without saying anything. It niggled at the back of her mind, making it hard for her to concentrate. By the time she made it home that night, she barely remembered anything she'd done or said all day. When she heard Drew's key turn in the front door, she had to force herself to stay where she was, even as the door closed behind him. Leaning her weight on one elbow on the kitchen countertop, she flipped to the next page in the magazine and called out. "Hey baby, I missed you when you left the hospital today."

A shadow fell over the pages in front of her and the same burst of happiness she always experienced when he was nearby ran through her.

"I had a few things to take care of. Isn't this a tempting picture?" Drew's deep rumbling voice ran down her spine as his hands gripped her waist. "Do you have anything on underneath this t-shirt?" Without giving her time to answer, he added, "Wait. Is this my t-shirt?" He tugged at the collar, checking the size. "It is. Damn, that's sexy as hell."

"It's comfortable," she complained with no real heat. She wasn't wearing anything underneath, and she was waiting for the moment he discovered it. Gripping the counter on either side of her, he crowded her with his body. Touching his lips to the back of her neck, he spoke against her skin.

"I'm not bitching. It makes me feel like I've marked my territory." Goosebumps covered her entire body and her nipples hardened as she dropped her chin to her chest giving him more access to her neck. Her eyes landed on his hands. His knuckles were split and blood still oozed from the open wounds.

"Oh my gosh, Drew! Why didn't you wrap your hands today?" She grabbed him by the wrists, tugged him to the sink and shoved his hands under the tap. Turning the water on, she leaned closer to his wounds. "What were you thinking?" she asked when he didn't say anything. "All it would take is one fracture in the right spot to screw up your whole career."

"Aubree."

"I'm serious, Drew. You'd be crushed."

"Aubree."

"It would break my heart too because I know how much you love it."

"Aubree," he said louder. Cutting off her tirade, Drew pulled his hands away and switched the water off. Spinning her around, he forced her to pay attention to him. As soon as she met his gaze, she realized how serious he was, and she bit down on her tongue to keep from saying anything else. "I'll get hurt," he told her firmly. "I'll bleed and bruise. It's my job, but I can take it, and you have to trust me when I say I'm okay."

"You could wrap your damn hands," she grumbled unable to stop the words.

He smiled at her childish tone. "It won't happen again. I promise." His smile fell and the solemn expression dropped back into place. "I need to tell you something important." She felt sick at his tone. If he was done, then she really

185

wished she had more clothes on.

Shoring up her courage, Aubree gave him a short nod. "Okay."

Cupping her face between his hands, he held her stare while keeping her in place as if he feared she would look away. He didn't say anything and her nerves were ready to snap as panic settled in her gut. "You're killing me, Drew."

"I'm in love with you."

"What?"

"I love you," he said again. "Actually, it was pretty instantaneous, which is a concept I always thought was a bit ridiculous, but then I met you. There is nothing I wouldn't do for you or give you."

"I don't want anything else," she said, cutting him off. Tears pricked at the backs of her eyes, and she realized she was gripping his shirt between her hands as if she'd been trying to physically hold him to her side. Relaxing her hands, she smoothed them up his chest before circling his neck.

"Really? You don't want anything else from me?" The seriousness of his tone brought her fear back to the surface. "Because I want things from you. I want you to love me in return."

"I do," she said without hesitation, but his expression still didn't change.

"I want you to want things from me, not because you know I care so much for you I'll give you whatever you ask for, but because you love me and trust me enough to know I'll take care of you. Please tell me you want things from me too?"

The mixture of pain and honesty shining in Drew's eyes was killing Aubree. She didn't want him to hurt because she'd held back in any way. Nodding, she forced her teeth to unlock and allow her to speak.

"I want to know you'll never leave me. I need to know this is forever."

*

"Thank God," he said. Swooping in, he opened his mouth over hers, overwhelming her. As his tongue brushed hers, she met him stroke for stroke. Cupping her ass, he hauled her against his erection and tore his mouth away. "Fucking hell. There's nothing under this shirt. Don't want to wait," he said, lifting her feet from the floor. She automatically wrapped her legs around his waist. With a few short strides, Aubree found her back against the wall. Proving his strength, Drew easily held onto her with one hand as he reached over his head and pulled his shirt over his shoulders. She helped in the effort. Aubree didn't want a thing between her hands and his skin. Free of his shirt, Drew tore at the button of his jeans and in a matter of seconds, his shaft stretched her wide. The moment he was fully seated inside her, Drew froze and held her stare. A flush covered his cheeks, causing the gray of his eyes to stand out in stark comparison. He looked turned on and sexy but also filled to the brim with emotion.

"You're not wearing a condom," she pointed out.

"Does it matter?"

The question gave her pause. She recognized they'd reached a pivotal moment in their relationship. "Only if you don't want children," she pointed out.

He rocked against her, stealing her breath. "I want it all with you, kids, marriage, the whole thing."

"You're beautiful," she said before she could stop herself. She tightened her inner walls around his cock. "I think you could make me come by doing nothing more than looking at me."

"I'm always up for a challenge but tonight is not the night." Rolling his hips, Drew withdrew an inch before pumping inside her. The friction of their bodies pulled at her clit and she dropped her forehead to his shoulder focusing on the ecstasy pulsing through her. Staring down between their bodies, she watched as the muscles in his stomach bunched and rolled. She caught flashes of his dick, shining wet with her juices, as it moved in and out of her. The smell of his skin, the sight of their joined bodies, and the direct pressure to her most sensitive parts overloaded her senses.

Drew growled as the first spasms hit and her channel pulled at his cock greedily. She gasped as the orgasm ripped through her, digging her fingernails into Drew's skin and attempting to cling to the feeling as long as possible. Pressing her weight into the wall, Drew gripped her ass almost painfully with one hand as he buried the other in her hair. Pulling her mouth to his, he sucked hard on her tongue as he ground against her. A sound of pure male pleasure tore from his throat as he came.

Aubree's feet slipped to the floor and Drew held on until he knew she was steady. The moisture rolling down the inside of her thigh reminded Aubree of how connected they now were. Drew snagged the hem of her shirt and hauled the material over her head. Swiping the shirt up her thigh and between her legs, he helped clean up the mess he'd made. Even with all the things they'd done, it felt like the most intimate moment they'd ever shared. When their gazes collided, Aubree knew Drew felt the same.

"I have to get you cleaned up so you can get dressed."

"Why am I getting dressed?"

"Because you're marrying me tonight," he answered simply before adding, "and then you'll give me a list of toys Trina is allowed to have in her room because we have shopping to do."

Her heart squeezed in her chest and the oxygen in the room seemed too thin. "We're getting married tonight?"

"It's Vegas. I can marry you any time I'd like." He held her stare. "We could wait, but I don't want to. I'll feel the same way about you whether it's today or ten years from now so let me have this, okay?"

"I love you," Aubree whispered, unable to think of a single thing to say powerful enough to express how happy he always made her.

Drew settled his mouth on hers,

lingering for a moment before deepening their kiss. It was slow, sweet and powerful. When he pulled away, the playful Drew was back in place. "I'm hard work, but I'm worth it," he promised.

Chapter Eight

Ryan leaned against the pillar in front of Aubree's door, hoping the bite of brick into his skin would take away the picture of a broken and battered Max that was branded in his brain. When questioned by the police, he refused to release a name or description of his attacker. Instead, in spite of all the evidence to the contrary, Max claimed he'd fallen down the stairs outside the gym where they worked. With no witnesses, video footage or cooperation, there was nothing anyone could do. It didn't matter what Max said to anyone else because Ryan knew the truth.

They'd been wrong. The guilt eating at him each day sat as a heavy reminder in his gut. Aubree had deserved so much better than what they'd done to her. Ryan missed her with something he couldn't name. Perhaps it was a step beyond desperation. However, he'd never expected Max's reaction to the loss of Aubree from their lives. His slow spiral out of control coupled with daily visits to see Aubree at work—which he gathered didn't go well by Max's mood when he returned—seemed to take a toll on him. No matter how wrong they'd been or how desperate Max was to reclaim her, his punishment hadn't fit his crime.

To his aggravation, when he began searching for Drew, he ran up against brick walls at every turn. Switching tactics, Ryan decided Aubree was the best way to locate the missing fighter. Unfortunately, once again, there was nothing. His search ended when, after a visit to her work, he'd learned from one of the other nurses Aubree had taken a vacation. She was due back today and the two hours Ryan had spent waiting for Aubree to get home did nothing to cool his seething rage. When Drew's silver ultra-expensive sports car pulled up at the curb, a pulse beat at his brain. Life had denied Drew nothing, including the woman sitting in the passenger seat. The frustration from months of waiting to have Aubree to only be given a few short hours enjoying her body pooled together with Ryan's vehemence over Max's injuries until a red haze covered his vision.

The simmering anger, guilt and hurt he nursed brought him to his feet. The world seemed to slow around him as he moved toward the car. Drew lifted Aubree's hand to his mouth, holding her gaze as he pressed his lips to it before opening his door. Aubree didn't move and she kept her face averted as if she could no longer bear to look at him. It was one thing too many.

Springing forward, Ryan struck, aiming for Drew's jaw. At the last second, Drew pivoted to the left and Ryan's fist swiped at empty air. Aubree leapt from the car as Drew snagged Ryan's arm. His vise-like grip sent a sharp pain all the way through Ryan's body as Drew twisted until Ryan hit his knees.

"What the hell are you doing?"

Ignoring Aubree's screeched question, Ryan gasped against the pain as he fought Drew's hold, but the man didn't let up. Aubree attempted to push her way between them and Drew shoved him away. Shooting back to his feet, Ryan curled his fingers into a fist, preparing to strike again. Aubree stepped into his path. The giant fighter—who'd been seconds away from breaking Ryan's arm—was rendered helpless by the tiny blonde woman as she refused to budge.

Under any other circumstances, Ryan might've found Drew's reaction funny. His inner debate was written all over his face. Drew was big enough to physically move her out of the way, but obviously too intelligent to try. With her palm flattened against his chest, Aubree pushed until Drew's back was against the car. Ryan didn't kid himself. He knew the man could plow right through her. He'd allowed Aubree to intervene. His eyes, however, told Ryan a different story. Ryan held onto his life by Aubree's mercy alone. Apparently satisfied Drew would behave, Aubree turned her rage on him.

"I cannot believe your fucking nerve. After everything you've done, you come to my house and pull this shit."

"Ask him what he did to Max," Ryan said, interrupting her tirade. "Or do you already know?" he added, as another horrible thought hit him. He'd never considered her involvement, but then again, it had been her they'd hurt.

When Aubree's brow furrowed in confusion, a spike of triumph ran through him. He released a bitter laugh. "So, he hasn't told you, after all."

She glanced over her shoulder at Drew. "What about Max?" His eyes went flat and any doubts Ryan had over the identity of Max's attacker fled.

Ryan could feel his jaw ticking as he bit down on his anger. "He's been in the hospital for the past week. He was found unconscious behind the gym. He has a concussion, six broken ribs and a hairline fracture in his collarbone. His spleen ruptured and there was some other internal bruising. He's refusing to cooperate with the police and there is no evidence to point at anyone, but I know who he was supposed to meet there," Ryan said tilting his chin in Drew's direction. Aubree opened her mouth as if to defend him, but her teeth snapped together and she turned on Drew.

"Your knuckles."

The two words brought about a world of change in Drew's expression. Ryan was rendered speechless at the powerful emotion written on the man's face as he stared at Aubree. "He put his hands on you," Drew said between clenched teeth. His nostrils flared, and Ryan braced to intervene as Drew took a step in Aubree's direction, but he merely brushed Aubree's hair away from her face before gently taking it between his hands. "Nobody puts their hands on my wife. The thought of anyone hurting you..." He trailed off as if choking on his words and shook his head.

"Wait. What?" Ryan asked, grasping to absorb what he was hearing.

Aubree clutched Drew's shirt appearing almost desperate to hang onto him. "How did you—"

Drew cut his eyes in Ryan's direction. "There were tiny eyes watching."

"I didn't want you to know."

"You should have told me," Drew said, and even Ryan could hear the pain behind the statement. "I'm your husband. You should have trusted me to keep you safe."

"Hold on. Hold on," Ryan said, unable to stand any more. "Max hit you and you married this guy?" He shook his head in disbelief as the pair continued to ignore him, and Aubree's voice turned almost pleading.

"I trust you always with everything.

It was never about that."

"Then why didn't you say anything? The moment Max got physical, you should have come straight to me. Scratch that. The first time he showed up at your job, you should have said something."

Aubree reached up, touching his hands, before drawing them away from her face, and linking their fingers. At the move, Ryan caught a flash of her wedding ring and the air left his lungs. "You're everything to me," Aubree said. "Do you know what I would do if the roles were reversed?" She dropped her chin to her chest and took a deep breath before meeting Drew's eyes once more. Ryan almost took a step back at the fierce look on her face. "I would kill someone if they touched you. That's why I didn't say anything. I knew you would hurt him, but in the end, it would be you who would lose everything. I couldn't watch Max limp away while you lost your career and reputation. You're worth a hundred of him. How could I let such a thing happen?"

When Drew responded, his voice came out sounding as if he'd been chewing on gravel. "I love you more than any of those things. Don't ever keep something like this from me again."

After a moment, Aubree nodded and Drew's eyes fell closed showing his relief over her acquiescence. Shock sat heavily on Ryan. As much as he didn't want to believe what he was hearing, the truth was in the powerful emotions hanging in the air. Max had physically hurt Aubree in some way. Even though Ryan's mind rejected the notion, as her husband, Drew had done what he knew how to do to protect her.

Without a thought to his own safety, Ryan moved in and wrapped his arms around Aubree's shoulders before anyone could protest. "I didn't know. I swear," he told her quietly. He didn't wait for a response. Their once beautiful friendship was dead and nothing anyone said would change things. The single option he possessed was to walk away and hope, one day, Aubree would no longer hate him.

*

The muscles in Drew's chest flinched as he physically held himself back from ripping Ryan's arms away from Aubree's shoulders. The blank expression on her face kept him in check. She endured Ryan's touch but she didn't welcome it. Without another word, Ryan walked away and climbed inside the red Chevy Tahoe across the street. He didn't drive away. Drew had wasted no time marrying Aubree and after making good on his promise to give Trina an awesome Christmas, he'd stolen Aubree away for a full week of solitude. All the while, he'd hoped this problem would disappear before they returned, but if it didn't, then he'd spent a week of bliss with his new wife before serving whatever sentence he landed. In spite of everything, Drew was willing to meet Ryan halfway. If Aubree wanted to keep him as a friend, she could have him as a friend and nothing more, or Drew would kill him.

"Should I tell him there is no reason for him to leave?"

Aubree shook her head at Drew's question. "I don't want him here." Before he had time to enjoy his relief over her answer, tears filled her eyes, and Drew couldn't breathe any longer. With everything she'd been through, he'd never seen her cry, and Drew made a terrible discovery. He couldn't handle it.

"I'm so sorry," she gasped out. Drew wrapped his arms around Aubree, clutching her tightly to his chest in part for comfort but also because her tears scared the hell out of him. A shudder ran through her. "I can't believe Trina saw everything. I feel like such an awful person. I didn't know what to do. She must've been so scared."

Drew snorted. "You're not an awful person and you shouldn't worry so much about Trina. The fact she was the one who witnessed everything is the best thing that could have possibly happened to you. That little girl was planning Max's downfall like a pro. She'll give some man hell one of these days."

Aubree let out a watery laugh before sobering once more. "You really almost killed him." Drew's grip tightened even more until she gasped, reminding him of his strength, and he was forced to loosen his hold.

Rubbing his hands over her back, he did his best to make amends. "I'm sorry. Sometimes I forget how easily I could hurt you, but it's as if I think if I hold onto you tight enough, then it will keep you with me once you figure out I'm too much of everything. It scares the hell out of me to think I might wake up from this dream and find you gone."

"Not happening," she said sounding fierce. He kissed the top of her head to let her know how much her words meant to him.

"I need you to know, I did try to do things differently. If I'd gone straight to Max after leaving the hospital, I would've killed him. Of that, I have no doubts.

Instead, I tried to calm down, and I went to see my dad."

Aubree pulled back and met his gaze appearing shocked. "You did?"

Drew slowly nodded. "At first, I thought I'd let Max have his way, and then maybe I wouldn't be as angry when I went to see him." Drew scrubbed his hand across the back of his head. "I know it doesn't make sense, but I guess I thought it would take the fear out of my anger. I didn't want him to ever come to you with anything again, but it did nothing but give me more time to stew over it. I kept picturing him—" Drew broke off, unable to give a voice to the things he saw inside his mind. Aubree attempted to soothe him with her touch. She smoothed her hands over his chest before moving to his shoulders and down his arms then repeating the motion. The sun glimmered off the diamond on her finger. He'd bought her the ring while they'd been in Monterey. He covered her hand with his, holding it in place against his chest. Her eyes were red-rimmed but dry and the blue of her irises stood out even brighter than usual. A thousand worries over how she might feel about him now rushed to the surface. However, after a moment of simply watching her, a tiny smile touched her lips. He knew they'd be okay.

"Just so you know, being married to me is a huge responsibility. I have expectations."

Aubree pressed her lips together, but in spite of her best efforts, a dimple appeared in the corner of her mouth. After a moment, she managed to rearrange her features into a serious expression. "Is that so? Well, this I have to hear."

He bit back a laugh at her tone and

barely managed a solemn nod. "I fully expect you to let me have my way in all things. In exchange for your cooperation, I promise to be the biggest freak in bed you've ever heard of."

A chuckle escaped Aubree before her eyes turned calculating. She closed the space between them, pressing her body against his. "Don't think I won't call you on your boast. I totally have a few ideas."

"I knew you would," he said, lowering his mouth to hers.

* * * * *

It took Ryan fifteen minutes to decide what to do. He'd exaggerated a bit when he explained Max's hospital stay to Aubree, not about the extent of his injuries, but Max had gone home the day before yesterday.

Turning the key in the ignition,

Ryan pulled away from the curb. His anger over the knowledge of what had really happened the night of Max's attack carried him all the way to the front door of the apartment he shared with the man filling his thoughts. The moment he stepped through the entryway, all Ryan felt was disappointment. Wearing a white cotton t-shirt and a loose pair of workout shorts, Max was sprawled out across the couch nursing his injuries, as he'd been instructed to do for the next four weeks.

Ryan realized in that moment, exactly how much he'd done for their friendship. He'd lied, schemed, hurt people he cared about and broken the law. After all those things, Max couldn't even be honest with him.

Kicking the door closed behind him, Ryan tossed his keys on the table before moving to stand over the man he suddenly felt he knew nothing about. The look of resignation on Max's face said more than anything else could have, as he waited silently for Ryan to explode. Instead, he sat down on the edge of the coffee table near Max's head, bracing his elbows on his knees while trying to decide what to say. Unable to think of a single thing that would define how he felt, Ryan settled on simply wanting to hear the truth.

"I just had an interesting chat with Drew." Max looked away, confirming his guilt. "Tell me," Ryan demanded, hearing the bite in his own words.

Max kept his eyes locked on the corner of the room as he cleared his throat uncomfortably. He opened his mouth, but no sound emerged. He lifted his hands in a helpless gesture before dropping them again. "I wanted my dad to get the closure he needed, and it was important to me for you to have the woman who means so much to you. I've spent so much fucking time trying to give everyone everything while pretending like it means nothing to me." Max gestured helplessly again as if he didn't know how to explain. "I begged Aubree to talk to Drew. She told me she was in love with him and wouldn't use his feelings for her against him. I saw everything slipping away. I kind of snapped, and it was like I wasn't me any longer. I pushed her and she hit her head." Max's eyes fell closed and Ryan could feel the man's disgust in himself. "The way she looked at me." Falling silent, Max shook his head. After a moment, he cleared his throat again. "Anyhow, when I agreed to meet Drew behind the club, I took one look in his eyes, and I thought, thank God I don't have to do this anymore. Unfortunately, I woke up in the hospital and realized it'll never end. For the rest of my life, I'll have to wake up feeling this way. I'll have to watch you…"

Max didn't finish. Ryan stared at the fading bruises on the left side of Max's face and contemplated making the right side match. "Really, Max? What the fuck?" He exploded before he realized it would happen. "Is she that important to you? Did losing Aubree mean so much? Does it mean everything to you for your father to get the chance to assuage his guilt over his mistakes that you would do this to yourself?"

A sad smile touched Max's lips, taking Ryan by surprise. "You're so fucking blind. I mean seriously God damn stupid blind," Max said with a snort. "I don't want Aubree at all."

Ryan couldn't do anything except stare at Max in disbelief. A thousand arguments came to mind. As he tried to decide which one to use first, he was blasted by the memory of the night they spent with Aubree. Her tight heat surrounded his cock while her cries of pleasure filled his ears. Her wet blonde hair clung to her chest as she rested her head against Max's shoulder. The closed expression Ryan was accustomed to seeing on Max's face was gone as he rocked against her from behind. A flush rode high on Max's cheeks and his lips parted on a gasp. He was the ultimate picture of aroused male, moments away from release. His eyes— Ryan viciously cut off the memory. He couldn't shut out the man who was silently watching him now. Max was right. He was so fucking blind.

"Why didn't you say anything?"

Max looked away at the question. "What would you have had me say?"

"Anything," Ryan answered immediately before his anger caught up with him and he added, "Anything at all would've been better than this fucking silence. Did you really think you couldn't say a single goddamn thing to me?"

Showing some life for the first time since Ryan walked through the door, Max met his gaze, and his eyes shined with fury. "And what, Ryan? What damn difference would it have made?"

Something inside Ryan snapped in the face of Max's anger. "This," he growled, pushing away from the table and snagging Max by the neck. Ryan caught a flash of surprise passing over Max's features, as he yanked him forward, and opened his mouth over his. It wasn't the first time they'd kissed. Just as Aubree wasn't the first woman they'd shared, but it had always been more of a heat of the moment, "everyone in this bed right now is turned on" sort of thing. This was different. This was Ryan accepting all the things he'd refused to see over the years. The desperation he'd felt to have Aubree was his need to have her as an excuse for what he really wanted. A sound vibrated from the back of Max's throat causing Ryan to go hard. He'd forgotten, or purposely blocked out, the memory of Max's taste. Now he couldn't get enough. Tightening his hold on the base of Max's neck, Ryan swore he felt his jaw crack as he went at Max's mouth.

Max gave back as good as he got until he attempted to drag Ryan even closer. He gasped in pain. Ryan jerked away. "Fuck. I forgot."

"Don't care," Max said between deep breaths as if attempting to push past his injuries.

"I care. I don't ever want to hurt you." Ryan held Max's stare trying to make him understand exactly how much he meant the words. In spite of the deep incision down the center of his abdomen and the cracked collarbone, Max's eyes were completely focused. "Damn. I forgot what it was like to have your full attention," Ryan breathed. Gripping the back of the couch to keep from leaning too much weight on Max's wounds, he dipped his head again, capturing Max's lips once more. He needed to leave the man alone and let him recover from his injuries. Ryan realized he simply wasn't capable of it as he sank his teeth into Max's bottom lip.

Max buried his hand in Ryan's hair, growling against his mouth. "To hell with this babying me shit. I'm not dead yet."

"Fuck you, you bastard. You don't get to leave me," Ryan argued, giving in to his anger over Max wanting Drew to kill him.

Max snorted. "Well, you're doing a pretty good job of trying to kill me now. At least take this fucking shirt off." Ryan leaned away, pulling the shirt over his head. Amber irises moved over his body, pausing at each of Ryan's tattoos, and his dick throbbed at the way Max was looking at him. "I changed my mind. Put it back on."

A husky laugh fell from Ryan's lips as he recognized exactly how turned on Max was. "No."

Max's nostrils flared as he took a steadying breath. The muscle in his jaw ticked. Unable to resist tormenting him further, Ryan swooped in again before he could argue. Max met him halfway. He sucked on Ryan's tongue in such a way that Ryan's balls drew up tight and he wondered if he would come from their kiss alone. Without giving Max any warning, Ryan reached down, and shoved his hand inside the workout shorts. As he slid his fingers down the silky skin of Max's erection, he groaned and Ryan stroked his shaft swearing the pleasure was his own. Tearing his mouth away, Max gulped for air. "Damn you. I have four more weeks of this torture."

Even as Ryan felt the evil grin stretch across his face, he couldn't stop it from forming, and he set a steady pace. Squeezing lightly each time he neared the tip of Max's cock, he savored the tiny drops of moisture escaping there. "Do you doubt my inventiveness?"

Max covered Ryan's hand halting his progress, and the intense look on his face somehow managed to become even more so. "I'm not trying to play games with you, Ryan."

Ryan brushed his thumb along his shaft, making sure he didn't forget where they left off as he seized Max's attention. Holding nothing back, Ryan let it all show in his eyes. "Tell me I'm playing," he dared him. Max's grip loosened on his hand but he didn't pull away. "Let me have this," he begged, and Max's eyes fell closed as Ryan dropped his head, nipping at his bottom lip again. "Let me watch you come unglued and know this one time it's for me alone."

Max's hand slipped away giving Ryan free rein over his body. "It's always been you and no one else."

The End

Keep an eye out for book 2, Undaunted (http://mybook.to/Undaunted).

Author Bio

Charity Parkerson is an award winning and multi-published author with several companies. Born with no filter from her brain to her mouth, she decided to take this odd quirk and insert it in her characters.

*2015 Readers' Favorite Award Winner
*Winner of 2, 2014 Readers' Favorite Awards
*2015 Passionate Plume Award Finalist
*2013 Readers' Favorite Award Winner
*2013 Reviewers' Choice Award Winner
*2012 ARRA Finalist for Favorite Paranormal Romance
*Five-time winner of The Mistress of the Darkpath

Connect with her online:

--Website: charityparkerson.com
--Facebook:
facebook.com/authorCharityParkerson
facebook.com/TheMenofSin
--Twitter: twitter.com/CharityParkerso